Other 1632 Universe Publications

*1*632 by Eric Flint created the universe. Free download available at Baen.com/1632.html. All listed books available at Baen.com.

Short-List of Titles to Jump into the Series:

Ring of Fire anthology edited by Eric Flint

1633 by Eric Flint and David Weber

1634: The Baltic War by Eric Flint and David Weber

All books available through Baen.com, booksellers, and used bookstores.

Also Available:

Grantville Gazette Volumes 1 – 102, magazine edited by Eric Flint, Paula Goodlett, Walt Boyes, Bjorn Hasseler. Available on 1632Magazine.com.

1632 Universe novels and "Eric Flint, Ring of Fire Series" on Baen.com

Forthcoming:

October 2024: *1635: The Weaver's Code* by Eric Flint and Jody Lynn Nye

Ongoing: Baen is re-releasing select 1632 books originally released by Eric Flint's Ring of Fire Press, starting with Bjorn Hasseler's NESS books. Please check the Baen.com e-arc bundles and new releases regularly!

Odd numbered months: New issues of Eric Flint's 1632 & Beyond

1632 & Beyond Issue 6

1632 and Beyond, Virginia DeMarce, Robert E. Waters, Terry Howard, Tim Sayeau, Iver P. Cooper

Flint's Shards, Inc.

ERIC FLINT'S 1632 & BEYOND ISSUE #6

Editor-in-Chief Bjorn Hasseler
Editor and Webmaster Bethanne Kim
Editor Chuck Thompson
Cover Artwork by Garrett W. Vance
Art Director Garrett W. Vance

1. Science Fiction-Alternate History
2. Science Fiction-Time Travel

eBook ISBN: 9781962398107
Paperback ISBN: 978-1-962398-11-4

Distributed by Flint's Shards Inc.
339 Heyward Street, #200
Columbia, SC 29201

Contents

Eric Flint's 1632 & Beyond Issue 6   1

Magdeburg Messenger
1632 Fiction

1. Passing Fair   5
   Virginia DeMarce

2. From Cramps To Matrimony   47
   Terry Howard

3. Cassini Runs Home   65
   Robert E. Waters

4. A Guest At The New Year   115
   Tim Sayeau

The State Library Papers
1632 Non-Fiction

5. Buzz! Beekeeping in the 1632 Universe, Part 2   129
   Iver P. Cooper

News and New Books
Available Now and Coming Soon

   Inside Baseball   147
   Bjorn Hasseler

Available Now 149

The Trouble with Huguenots, The Carthaginian Crisis, Legions of Pestilence, Security Solutions, Security Threats, Missions of Security

Coming Soon 163

Things Could be Worse, Designed to Fail, 1635: The Weaver's Code

Connect with Eric Flint's 1632 & Beyond 171

Eric Flint's 1632 & Beyond Issue 6

The Magdeburg Messenger

(1632 Fiction)

This issue's cover art comes from "Passing Fair" by Virginia DeMarce. That term is both the source of confusion between up-timers and down-timers and something of a pun—but also a matter about which reasonable people can sharply disagree.

Terry Howard's "From Cramps To Matrimony" shows how technology has consequences. Specialty teas in Grantville lead to socioeconomic tension in Mecklenburg Province.

Robert E. Waters concludes his cycle of baseball stories with "Cassini Runs Home." It's about much more than the team's season.

"A Guest At The New Year" by Tim Sayeau is a wonderfully creative story. Of all the future knowledge that an up-timer could provide a down-timer, this probably wasn't on your list at all.

State Library Papers

(1632 Non-Fiction)

The second part of Iver P. Cooper's article on beekeeping and its potential in the new timeline addresses transplanting bees and beekeeping law..

Magdeburg Messenger
1632 Fiction

Flint's Shards, Inc.

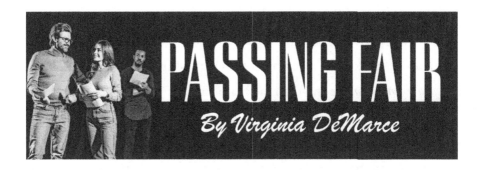

Passing Fair

Virginia DeMarce

E ditor's Note: References are given at the end of the story.

Grantville, SoTF
November 1636

"Where's Master Marmion?" Renee Carson demanded

The rest of the high school's advanced drama class (elective; juniors and seniors only; may be repeated for credit a second year; non-mandatory option for participation with community theater and/or local professional theater groups; pairing with speech/debate/forensics advised for maximum benefit) produced uniformly blank expressions.

Amalia Hartmann arrived puffing. "Down in the auditorium, arguing with Master Massinger. And with my brother Leonhard. And with Dick Quiney. And with Master Ashmead."

"Scheduling, what else? Since Massinger is taking his company to Magdeburg next month, he wants to fit in another play here before he leaves, even though every available night is filled up."

"He's an arrogant..."

"No, not really. His group really is the best. Or, at least, the most fun."

Salome Selfisch shook her head. "I thought it was rude of Master Massinger to make that sweeping bow to Frau Mundell when they finished *Measure for Measure* and then call her plain."

"He did no such thing!" Natasha Clinter jumped up.

By the time Shackerly Marmion arrived, playwright and (perforce, if he wished to continue to eat) teacher of Grantville's youth, the classroom had degenerated into a shouting match.

"How so, Miss Selfisch? Precisely what did he say?"

"He said that she was 'passing fair.'"

Marmion sighed and thought that it was often harder to negotiate the differences between up-time and down-time English than it was to generate comprehension between either form of English and German—any form of German, Amideutsch included. All of which tended to be used in every class he taught, every hour of the school day. Not to mention at the community theater in the evenings.

"'Passing fair' doesn't mean plain; it means very beautiful."

"That can't be right," Melissa Higgenbottom objected.

"Why not?"

"I get 'fair.' That means good-looking. But 'passing' means barely scraping along. Like when someone asks you how you did on a test, and you answer that you got a passing grade. Which means that it wasn't anything to brag about."

"No," Marmion said. "This is 'passing' as in 'surpassing.' Before tomorrow's class, all of you look that up in the dictionary, find out why, and write down the definition."

This resulted in some dissatisfied scribbling in notebooks.

"Now, will the class please come to order. Yesterday, we were discussing the Aristotelian unities..."

The debate carried over into the cafeteria at lunch. Salome Selfisch was nothing if not stubborn. "It still sounded as if he was calling her homely."

"Mrs. Mundell isn't homely. Not if you take that to mean ugly, and be careful in front of Mr. Marmion or he'll make us look that up and write out the definition, too." Hans Hardy (formerly Hans Marbacher) had minimal enthusiasm for written assignments.

"She's not 'surpassingly beautiful' either, though." Jim Abodeely was of the opinion that his status as younger brother of one of Bitsy Matowski's lead ballerinas made him a connoisseur of feminine pulchritude.

"Master Massinger was using a superlative. As a compliment," Hans retorted.

"But 'passing' fair is what she is. What I thought it meant, I mean," Salome persisted. "She's just kind of ordinary looking. Her face is round, she's got light brown hair—well, with some gray in it, now—and hazel eyes and generally nothing special."

Salome had dark hair, bright blue eyes, and, with the indulgence of her sister-in-law Mindy Hill, who was a beautician at Carole's, spent quite a bit of time and money on an effort to achieve the "something special" level.

"Mr. Mundell must have thought she was cute, twenty years ago, or he wouldn't have married her." Hans admired Salome—who wouldn't?—but was at the stage where he was inclined to think that if someone was female and breathed, she was attractive.

"Men marry a lot of women who aren't particularly pretty," Jim said. "Just look around you. Somebody married Mrs. Bellamy or she wouldn't be *Mrs.* Bellamy."

Hans considered this. All of them had taken either algebra or geometry from Mrs. Bellamy. Following debate class procedure, he bowed and stated, "I concede your point."

Grantville, SoTF
January 1637

Lorrie Mundell laid the letter opener down on the kitchen table. "I can tell you exactly who it's from! It's from someone who owns a manual typewriter and doesn't have the guts to put his or her return address on the envelope. An up-time envelope, not one of the standard business sizes. Probably originally from a greeting card."

She pushed the remnant of her breakfast back and flattened the sheet of paper that the envelope contained out on the table so the four boys could see it.

"Containing a screed, also typed, copying one of those pamphlets that the American Tract Society used to distribute. Another diatribe on the un-Christian evils of the theater."

"Look, Mom." Mike, her older son, gobbled the last bite of scrambled eggs on his plate.

"Don't talk with your mouth full." Lorrie's response was automatic, even if Mike had recently passed the birthday that made him a legal adult in the SoTF.

Zacharias Schaupp, the older of her two foster sons, who had also recently passed that landmark birthday, started to reach for it.

"Don't," his brother Wolfgang said. "We ought to take it to the police and get it fingerprinted."

"For whose fingerprints?" That was Jim, her younger son. "It's been through the Post Office. Someone's sorted it. Someone's delivered it." He reached for the sausage gravy and ladled a generous helping on top of the four biscuit halves on his plate. "There's nothing the police could do, anyway. Whoever sends these doesn't make threats—not direct ones. It's just more of the 'going to the movies is bad for your soul' stuff. They didn't even approve of 'sword-and-sandal flicks,' much less secular plays live on stage."

"Of *what*?" Zacharias asked.

"Movies like *Quo Vadis. Ben Hur*," Lorrie explained.

"All the Moses stuff, like the *Ten Commandments*," Jim added. "Movies that Brother Curtis says were 'full of least common denominator Christianity and uplifting moral platitudes,' and I can't say that he's wrong."

"I hate to think that any of these would be coming from our church," Lorrie said.

She still thought of the Church of Christ as her church, even though she didn't attend much. Hadn't for a long time.

"You can't say that Brother Curtis is really wrong about that, even if he does tend to use phrases like, 'the commodification of religion' when he talks about those movies from the 1950s," Lorrie continued. "Brother Curtis isn't from right around here—his family's from the county, but not from Grantville. When Mrs. Curtis married him, some of the elders were a little doubtful about foreigners." She grinned. "Doug Curtis is very earnest and sincere, though. He wouldn't hold with sending people unpleasant tracts in anonymous envelopes. Not even to people who are involved in Philip Massinger's theater troupe and act in plays that say rude things about Lutheran and Episcopalian bishops."

She looked at the two Schaupp boys. "Not even to foreigners, and that's not pointed at you two because you're down-timers. I was born in Berea, Kentucky, myself. By the standards of a lot of folks in Grantville, that was pretty foreign, even though both my parents grew up not too far from

Grantville, out in the county. But when George found me and brought me back, we were both working out in South Dakota. Of course, it didn't help that he was divorced from what the local folks considered to be a perfectly good Grantville girl. Bill Slater's sister Linda was his first wife. She was left up-time."

"From a personal point of view," Mike commented, "I'm just as glad that Dad found you, given that I wouldn't exist otherwise, and neither would Jim." He grabbed the last biscuit, split it, put a sausage between the halves, and jammed the entire thing into his mouth. "Get a move on, guys. There are sets to construct before we manage to get ourselves packed up and moved to Butzbach to visit Master Massinger's friend."

They hammered and painted all day. The cast showed up to rehearse after school was out. They had to rehearse after school got out, given that several of the players were high school students and Mr. Marmion, the director, was a teacher.

"This is the sort of thing the letter says." Zacharias Schaupp waved a scrap of paper during the first break. "I copied it when I went home for lunch."

But, by some strange concurrence of circumstances, this evil, sinful and pestiferous as it evidently is, has crept, under a sort of disguise, into the Church of Christ; and has come to be considered by many, as an amusement lawful for Christians! With respect to most other sins which we are in the habit of reproving, they are freely and generally acknowledged to be such; and when any of those who belong to the communion of our churches fall into them, they are dealt with as circumstances require. But we have here the strange phenomenon of a great and crying sin, which some professed Christians not only indulge—but which they openly endeavor to justify; to which they freely introduce their children; and, as if this were not enough, in behalf of which they take serious offence when the ministers of Christ speak of it in the terms which it deserves. Rely upon it, reader, this practice will not stand the test of examination. It is corrupt and indefensible throughout; and the more speedily you become convinced of this, and act accordingly, the better will it be for yourself, and the better for society.

February 1637

Lorrie wriggled until the back of her neck was cushioned just right on the edge of the basin. "Hot water," she directed. "Really hot, please. Massage my scalp hard."

Carole Trelli laughed. "Some things never change."

"I don't have all that many self-indulgences. I don't want to give this one up. I'm willing to sacrifice a lot, if I have to, even though I hope I don't have to, but not getting my hair done." Lorrie giggled.

Massinger's Men were off to Butzbach. With the sudden departure from her house of four hungry, noisy, teenage boys, Lorrie was feeling simultaneously a bit empty-nested from missing them and profoundly happy for not having to feed them.

Although she had slipped Master Massinger a bit of a subsidy to go toward the feeding costs, just in case Landgrave Philipp didn't cover them all.

"What I need," she said, "is a hobby. Or something to do, at least. Maybe I should volunteer for something."

"You were acting for Massinger, weren't you?" asked Stephanie Turski in the next chair. She taught art at the high school, but her M.A. in film studies led her to keep her finger on the pulse of every group that was putting on plays in Grantville.

"Only a couple of times, and just as a favor to the boys. I don't love being in front of an audience the way George does."

"Marmion could probably use you in community theater, though."

"Maybe you need grandchildren."

"Give me a break! Mike and Jim aren't old enough to settle down. Not even close. If either of them got a girl pregnant now, it would be a 'have to' wedding, and I'm not a fan of those. Besides, I think I've probably hatched a few plays. Intellectual grandchildren, so to speak. Or artistic grandchildren."

"What?"

"I gave Tom Quiney some books before they left. The way they've been cribbing from Broadway musicals this last year, I figured he could steal some plots. Frank Yerby. Thomas B. Costain. Those guys?"

"I have no idea who they are," Carole admitted.

"Not sword and sorcery." Lorrie took a minute to think. "No sorcery at all. Sort of historical fiction. Swash and buckle. Besieged castles. Pirate ships. Sword fights. Damsels in distress." She giggled again. "Buxom damsels, if you go by the cover illustrations. The Yerby books belonged to my dad. Yerby lived a long time after Dad died, and kept on writing. But the pile I gave to Tom Quiney had *The Golden Hawk* and *The Saracen Blade*. Those ought to capture his imagination. Tom's still in his teens, even if he is the grandson of William Shakespeare and already a playwright. I think that Tom will value the Yerby novels more than either of my own kids ever would. I know those two stories can be dramatized, because they both got made into movies back in the 1950s."

Lorrie laughed. "I added a couple of Thomas B. Costain's books to the box, because when I asked Tom, he said he hadn't come across them. There are enough words in *The Black Rose* to fertilize a half-dozen 'historical' plays. Those came from my Grandpa Jerry; his wife Pansy gave them to

Ma after he died. He never went to college, in spite of all the nagging the family did; he was a short order cook. Quite a reader, though. I think he read everything that Louis L'Amour ever wrote."

"The Yerby books are about all I had of Dad's, so I hope that Tom takes good care of them. He—Dad, that is; not Tom—died so young, twenty-six years old, just a year after I was born. It wasn't that Ma didn't keep much. It was that he didn't have much."

To say in Carole's—with every stand busy and every ear listening—that he had died in a one-car DUI would have been TMI and then some.

"Volunteer!" Stephanie said. "Come on over to the school after you get off work tomorrow. We'll find something to fill up your spare time."

* * *

Shackerly Marmion sipped on the brewed cacao that the Sternbock Coffee House now offered as an alternative form of outrageously expensive consumable hot liquid to those who could not seem to develop a taste for real coffee. "This tract you are talking about sounds very Puritan. I would look among the Presbyterians for the sender, if I were Mistress Mundell."

"But there are oceans and oceans of Christian plays," Melissa Higginbottom objected. "What about that passion play at Oberammergau that everyone was talking about a couple of years ago—whether it would ever happen or not, because there wasn't a plague epidemic in Bavaria the year that there was one up-time."

"For that matter," Natasha Clinter said, "what about Christmas programs? Or nativity scenes? I mean, our church doesn't do them..." Like the Mundells, the Clinters were Church of Christ people—somewhat more meaningfully so. "We don't even use instrumental music in the services. It's all *a capella* hymn singing. But outside of church, I mean, Dad's the principal at the middle school, and they put on programs there. I was in some of them before I started high school. There used to be more before

Mrs. Nelson moved to Quedlinburg, but I don't remember that any of the elders came up to him and said that school plays were the work of the devil. And now I'm taking drama. He doesn't have a problem with it."

"Or real plays?" Renee Carson contributed.

"Real plays?" Melissa folded up the waxed paper that had contained her sandwich and put it carefully in the brown paper sack. She would re-use them both. "What's unreal about the passion play at Oberammergau, since they did go ahead and put it on?"

"I mean plays like *The Crucible*. Arthur Miller was famous. *Murder in the Cathedral*. T.S Eliot was even more famous, up-time. We've studied both of those."

"Arthur Miller was famous because he shagged Marilyn Monroe," Jim Abodeely said.

Renee tossed a square of cheese at him. "Not just for that. And don't just look at Presbyterians. The Catholics did a lot of movie censorship. Mom has talked quite a bit about the Legion of Decency—you know, the thing that insisted that even married couples with kids had to sleep in twin beds in movie bedrooms. That lasted until after Mom was born—not by much, but it did. She was brought up Catholic, even if she isn't Catholic any more, so she knows."

Marmion stood up. "Break's over. I will ask Mistress Mundell if she will lend me that tract she received."

A few days later, in a letter directed to Magdeburg, he appealed to Frau Dunn, his predecessor at the high school, for a list of recommended reading, "for, although I consider myself competent to teach these children the art of acting and the dramatic literature of this day and age, I have no preparation whatsoever for addressing the questions that have been arising in the wake of young Master Quiney's *Baby Bishops* play. Nor am I even certain that doing so is included within my remit."

Amber Dunn's first thought was that this was certainly nothing new.

"I've run into some of this before," she wrote back. "Byron Higham, my first husband, was from Michigan, originally. I worked in community theater and semi-professional theater in Minneapolis—that is, or was, in Minnesota, not Michigan—for fifteen years while I was married to him, before I divorced him, got my teaching credentials, and moved back to Grantville.

"I'm inclined to agree with you that the objections are most likely to be coming from people with Calvinist backgrounds. The Legion of Decency and organizations like that wanted to censor what plays and movies could show, but they didn't want to abolish them, up-time, any more than the Catholics do here down-time. Just think of those massive spectacles that the Jesuits put on.

"With the Calvinists, though—it's not just that they, like your English Puritans, objected to things like cross-dressing, men wearing women's clothes, so boys could play female roles, because that wasn't a thing, up-time. It wasn't just that they thought actors and actresses were generally 'a licentious and profligate lot,' though most of them sure did! It wasn't even, mostly, that they thought going to plays and movies was a 'sinful waste of time,' as the author of that tract you enclosed in your letter put it. It wasn't even that going to shows brought 'decent' people into contact with the 'licentious and profligate' types. By the time I moved back to Grantville, a substantial number of the Reformed in the upper midwest were wrestling against such things as folks showing Dickens's *Christmas Carol* on videos in their own living rooms, parents and kids watching together. As I understood the underlying argument..."

* * *

"The author of that tract seems to think it's a sin to have an imagination." Jim Abodeely's tone of voice made it clear that he didn't agree.

"I'm not sure it's just imagining things," Salome said. "I think it's more that the author is against people pretending to be something that they aren't. He's saying that you shouldn't try to be something that you weren't created to be."

Renee Carson giggled. "It's just as well that whoever wrote them didn't realize that in England, for plays open to the public, boys play the female roles. He'd be shouting about drag queens. If you can shout on paper."

"He probably can," Jim answered. "Or put it in capital letters. Or bold type. Or italics. Or underline it."

"Like my cousin Maddy says," Natasha Clinter contributed, "sometimes she feels like a total hypocrite, studying to grow up and be a librarian like a good little girl, because the teachers say that she should, when she really isn't very much interested in libraries. Or at all interested in them, really."

As the spring dragged on—March was a thoroughly nasty month when it came to weather—there was more and more talk around Grantville about the revving up of the Anti-Slavery League's activity. They were even seeking to recruit participants for an expedition to Luanda.

In April, Lorrie got a letter from Jim in Butzbach. Some local busybody had started pompously prating that Wolfgang would need to go back to school when Massinger's Men returned to Grantville, because apprenticeships were just so *passé* these days. Wolfgang had threatened to run away if Lorrie made him go back to school.

She joined a committee on expanding "non-traditional curricula" in the public schools for those students who were actually high-school age (or even middle-school age) but didn't want to, or couldn't, go to school for various reasons.

Which was why Kirsten came running after her. "Brad wanted me to ask—can they have the committee meeting at your house tonight? The kids are sick and there's no such thing as an open room at any of the schools."

"Sure. I can cram six chairs around the kitchen table. Please tell people to come in the back, so they can kick their shoes off in the mud room. I've finally gotten the carpet halfway clean and would just as soon keep it that way until the boys come back."

"I hear you."

* * *

"Could I use the restroom?" Brad Laforrest asked.

"Sure—down the hallway to the front, and then left. There's a half-bath off that room, in what used to be a closet. They put it in for Donna before she died, so she didn't have to climb the stairs every time she needed to go."

He walked down the hallway, looked casually at a "photo family tree" on the wall, stopped, and looked again. And again, on his way back to the kitchen.

* * *

Even without Massinger's Men, Grantville had more live theater now than before the Ring of Fire. Lots more. Way more. There was something available almost every night. In December, when Massinger's Men were off in Magdeburg, they'd done *A Christmas Carol*. It wasn't just the high school drama class. There was a community theater group, too, with Shackerly Marmion directing it.

He was trying Oscar Wilde's *The Importance of Being Earnest* next. Mainly, he said, to find out whether or not he was capable of directing a play that had been written up-time.

"Not all the way up-time," Stephanie Turski said. But not to Marmion's face.

Lorrie was not all that into acting. Not the way the boys were involved with Massinger. They got that more from George, who was still off and away, doing important things in other places.

But she tried out. Mainly because she was so mad at whoever was sending her those anti-theater broadsides. She got the part of Lady Bracknell.

Most of the rest of the cast was from the advanced drama class at the high school.

* * *

"Mrs. Turski?" Salome Selfisch asked in art class.

"Yes?"

"You've seen these tracts against plays."

"Yes."

"What do you think?"

"They're outside anything in my previous experience."

Stephanie thought that ought to be noncommittal enough.

"Do you think we'll be blamed for them?"

"We? Who do you mean by 'we' in that question.

"Us. The down-timers. I know that a lot of the up-timers think...well, that we're sort of backwards. That they've landed in a primitive place. Who else are they likely to blame?"

"The language of the pamphlets is fairly clearly up-time English. Not really modern up-time English, but it would take a lot more effort than it would be worth, I think, for a down-timer to imitate it."

Salome nodded as she looked at her efforts to construct a mobile.

"I just thought I'd ask."

* * *

As Frau Dunn's letters continued, Marmion stood there at his desk, dumbfounded. On what possible basis could any rational scholar conclude that it was *per se* sinful to play a role...to pretend to be someone else?

Master Massinger and the Quiney brothers had repeatedly warned him, of course, that many of the up-timers were inclined to be prudish. This went far beyond prudishness. These authors defined drama itself as a sin—not anything that a particular play depicted, the things that the English government so loved to censor and use as excuses for closing the theaters when it was convenient for their lordships—but the very existence of drama. The better an actor was, the more thoroughly he subsumed himself and assumed the personality of another—which violated God's will for who he was to be and defied the stamp that God himself had put upon an individual when creating him. The actor would either become polluted, sinking to the level of the villain he was depicting, or, alternatively, become guilty of intolerable presumption in attempting to portray the motivations of and relationship with God experienced by a man of holy life—such as Moses, for example—especially if he were not such a man himself. Which an actor was not likely to be (see above for 'licentious and profligate').

It took quite a lot to shock Shackerley Marmion.

Amber Dunn's description of these up-time criticisms of the theater managed it. It was clear that the Puritan critics of the theater in his own day had an extraordinarily tenacious effect.

Even if Frau Dunn did end the letter by saying that she rather doubted that there was anyone in Grantville who was even familiar with the details of such theories, much less actively subscribing to them, and the person sending the tracts to Frau Mundell probably was just a run-of-the-mill troublemaker—list of recommended reading enclosed for his use.

Marmion re-read the pertinent paragraphs in Frau Dunn's most recent letter. All this went far beyond any criticism of drama that Plato had made, although Plato had been, among the ancients, harsh enough. Far beyond what Saint Augustine of Hippo had said. For that, far beyond what any of the parishioners drinking coffee and eating cookies after the services at St. Alfred's Episcopal Church had said about Tom Quiney's *Baby Bishops* play.

* * *

If Marmion had thought to consult Victor Saluzzo, the principal at the high school (Catholic), he would have been advised not to do it.

If Marmion had thought to consult Archie Clinter, the principal at the middle school (Church of Christ), he would have been advised not to do it.

If Marmion had thought to consult Philip Massinger, happily producing repertoire in a small castle in Butzbach while storing up a set of fresh scripts, he would have been advised not to do it.

If he had consulted Amber Dunn, he would have been *strongly* advised not to do it, on the grounds of not asking for trouble.

He didn't consult any of them.

After all, he wouldn't be using school facilities. It wouldn't be on school time.

Every Grantville newspaper had an advertisement in a neatly outlined black box announcing a public debate on the merits of the dramatic arts.

There were ads on the Voice of America, as well.

Nicole Hawkins had been happy to agree that Renee should take the "pro" side. Nicole was all in favor of forensics; Renee was turning into a competent debater; her mom was proud of her.

It hadn't been so easy for him to find a student willing to present the "con" arguments—given that his acquaintances were mainly limited to those students who wanted to take drama and whose parents were willing for them to enroll in drama.

Until Anthony Green volunteered. Anthony had graduated in the accelerated program the previous spring and joined his older brother Allen at the university in Jena.

"Pete and repeat," had been his sour comment to Renee at the time. "Of course I can't go somewhere that Allen hasn't already gone or do something that Allen hasn't already done."

Now he said, "Honestly, when you come down to it, I suspect that Dad has his own doubts about the acceptability of movies and plays, and he's on the more intellectual end of being a Baptist. You could probably find a batch of people at First Baptist who would be more than happy to argue the 'con' side, and not just to make the debate work."

In the two weeks between the publication of the first advertisements and the holding of the debate, it turned out that—*several*—of the up-time Protestants had at least occasional uneasy feelings that even if they loved plays and movies, their grandparents would have most certainly disapproved. Or their great-grandparents. Or some ancestor, back in the day, when people were more virtuous than they had become in these parlous modern times.

At the Church of Christ, Doug Curtis observed to his wife Eloise that he had a bad feeling about this. She laughed at the movie reference and said she was glad that Doug Jr. was a couple of years too old to have gotten himself involved, being safely off fighting the plague in the Province of the Main.

For certain values of "safe," but right at the moment, he was less likely to be finding trouble while he was enforcing quarantines in Mainz than he would if he were debating about drama in Grantville.

"Did Anthony really have to do this?" Al Green asked his wife Claudette. "I could have done without this right now."

"He didn't have to, but he did," Claudette answered. She was a practical woman. "At least we're up here on the hill, at the Institute, rather than still down at First Baptist."

The debate was unexpectedly well-attended, garnering quite a bit of press coverage.

Anthony threw himself into his role with flourishes. Quite dramatic ones. Largely thanks to the anonymous donor of another page of some tract:

Attendant on the theater, did you ever hear of that awful catastrophe which caused the tears of so many to flow, a few years since, in one of our cities—when a theater, in the midst of its performances, and unusually crowded, was destroyed by fire—and seventy-five people perished in the flames? Did you ever hear of that heart-rending scene? Did you ever try to image to yourself how you would have felt, if you had been there? Think of A THEATER IN FLAMES! and ask whether you would be willing to meet death in a playhouse—to pass, as it were in a moment, from all the polluted vanities of such company, and such a scene—to the immediate presence of a holy God! How tremendous the thought! yet no one can tell that a like calamity may not happen at any time when he allows himself to be present in such a place. But, fellow-mortal, if you never should see a theater in flames, you will see a WORLD IN FLAMES, and a holy Judge descending to his "great white throne;" and "the heavens and the earth passing away, that there shall be no place found for them." And you shall see "many great men, and rich men, and mighty men, hiding themselves in the dens, and in the rocks of the mountains; saying to the mountains and rocks, Fall upon us, and hide us from the face of Him who sits on the throne, and from the wrath of the Lamb; for the great day of his wrath has come, and who shall be able to stand?" Will attendance on the theater, do you think, be a means of preparing any man to meet that Judge, and to stand the trial of that great day? May God, of his infinite mercy, open the eyes, and turn the hearts of infatuated men, that they may see their folly and danger before it is forever too late!

Quite a few people suspected him of satire, but most of those who came with the intent of supporting the hypothesis he was defending took his presentation quite seriously.

* * *

"Oscar Wilde is a bad influence! Lady Bracknell is an evil woman!" Lorrie flopped down on the increasingly worn vinyl of the reclining chair at Carole's. "The usual. If I had any idea what stupid old fart is spreading these pamphlets around, I'd give him the what-for! 'Lady Bracknell is an evil woman.' Too bad that Marmion didn't pick the Scottish play. That guy, whoever he is, should see me do Lady Macbeth."

That was too much, even for Lorrie's little temper tantrum. When Carole laughed, she laughed at herself.

"Actually, I'm no more capable of playing Lady Macbeth than I am of sprouting wings and flying to the moon. But I'd be willing to try, just for the sake of pissing this guy off even more. And I'm really glad that George is still out of town while this is going on. It would make him so mad."

* * *

The best way to describe how Bradley Laforrest was feeling was that he was stewing. Stewing to himself, for the time being. He was pretty sure that Lorrie Mundell was "passing."

And the Anti-Slavery League meetings often sort of wandered away from the topic of slavery to the topic of being black in Grantville. What was a black identity? How did you keep one? Especially fellows like Jason Smith and Tom Brumfield, who intended to be part of the Luanda expedition because they weren't tied down with wives and kids.

"What does being black mean to those guys, anyhow? There's no way that these young men will have had the same life experiences as if they had been reared in black households."

"Now, look here!" Joanie Smith exploded.

"Oh, I can see where Brad is coming from," Isaiah Avery said. "He's not by himself. It was in 1972, I think, that the National Association of Black Social Workers formally condemned interracial adoption. It was the same argument: the kids were "at risk" for developing a poor racial identity due to lack of contact with role models of the same race. That's when people who wanted kids started bringing them from Romania. Or Russia. Or China. Or any place that had more kids in orphanages than they could cope with. And what happened in the good old USA? Kids who could have been adopted were left to grow up in foster care and group homes."

"Do you think we don't know that?" Lacy Brumfield asked. "Why did we adopt Tommy? Well, blame me if you want to, but we wanted a healthy kid the second time. Hey, we knew when we adopted Sherry that she had juvenile diabetes. She was two years old already; because of it, she was 'hard to place.' The agency didn't soft-pedal it, and we took it on willingly. All the treks to doctors and hospitals, trying to get her insulin balanced and keep it that way. Then the other allergies that showed up, and the restrictions, so she couldn't eat a lot of things that other kids did. How much she was resenting it by the time she was ten or so—and, believe me, it didn't get any easier when she hit the teen years. And then the Ring of Fire, and she died that same year. Which we knew she would, once reality set in."

"Lacy..." Joanie said. "Maybe Brad and the rest don't really care..."

Lacy just kept going.

"But when we went to adopt again, a few years after Sherry, I just didn't have the strength to repeat that. I said to the lady from the agency, 'healthy, please God, just give me a healthy kid.' So they gave us Tommy, who's as healthy as they come. A kid who could play sports, a kid that Rick could volunteer to coach the teams he was on, be a Scout leader with. It only took a year or so for them to find him for us. He was eight years old and pretty much hating the whole world. I guess we were his last hope."

She paused a minute, looking at Isaiah. "You're right. The agency didn't make any bones about it: if they could have found a black family to adopt him, we wouldn't have gotten him. A few years later, we wouldn't have gotten him. Those placements, black or bi-racial kids in white homes, pretty much stopped by the 1990s."

"Ideology," Joanie snorted. "It's worse than religious fanaticism, if you ask me. But since we're on the topic, when we adopted Jason in '87, he'd been knocking around in foster care for five years. No permanent placement. They actually let us have him because we were adopting Jessica–they're half-siblings–she was two, but hadn't been freed up until then. When we were looking through the material from the agency, we discovered that he was out there—a half-brother—and told the social worker that we wanted him, too. It was against their policy, actually. Except that it's also policy to keep siblings together if they can, which made a problem for them, because Jessica isn't biracial; it was their birth mother who was white.

"And then, back in the '80s, there were a lot more black families in Grantville. Look at the class photos hanging in the entrance corridor at the high school, if you don't believe me." She waved her hand in the general direction of the high school.

"That out-migration didn't really start until the middle of the decade. Actually, right around the time that Rick and Lacy and us adopted. There were other black families in the schools, and then, all of a sudden, there weren't any. I won't pretend that it didn't cause problems, sometimes. Sometimes the other kids in the schools were pretty hostile."

Her smile was fierce. "You're a football guy, Brad. Think of it as Lacy and I formed a tight defensive alliance to protect Tom and Jason from the worst of it."

* * *

Joanie talked to Carole Trelli because Carole Trelli was born Carole Smith. She was Hank's sister. Joanie's sister-in-law. And Betty Avery's mother.

So Carole talked to Roberta Sutter when she came in for her regular appointment, because Roberta was the president of the Genealogical Society.

Roberta thought about it. "It's more complicated than you might think—this question of how much your ancestry determines who you are. You really ought to go to a genealogical society sometime, when there's a talk on tracing American Indian ancestry. Or, well, you know—you should have gone to one, up-time, when you could have.

"There was a great article written by a guy at the National Archives. He called it 'Wantabes and Outalucks.' Sometimes, it seemed like half the people in the country wanted to claim a Native American ancestor. You know, all those folks who think they have a Cherokee princess somewhere in the family tree, aside from the point that Cherokees didn't have princesses. Do you know what actual Cherokees say to that? 'If you haven't walked the walk, you shouldn't talk the talk.' As far as they're concerned, even if a person might have some remote Indian ancestry, unless you've grown up inside, with the reservation experience, you don't have any business claiming to be Native American."

* * *

Betty Trelli–Betty Avery, she was now–plopped into the chair at Carole's. "Thanks for staying late, Mom. God, but my hair is a mess. I pumped this afternoon and nursed Jasmine right before I left, so she should be good for three hours. Isaiah doesn't have a committee meeting for a change, so I didn't have to get a sitter."

Carole examined her third daughter's hair critically. "Mess" was accurate. Mid-winter dry straw. She pulled out the lanolin. "Let me condition that before I even shampoo it. I'll do your nails while we're waiting." She rubbed the salve in, then started filing and buffing.

"Has Isaiah said anything about..."

"The bee that Brad Laforrest has in his bonnet? Yeah."

"Do you..."

"Hey, I was interested in Isaiah for a couple of years before the Ring of Fire hit. And I'm honest enough with myself to admit that I'd probably never have done anything about it if we were still up-time. There were just too many complications for interracial couples. As soon as it got real that we were going to be stuck in the seventeenth century forever—right after the Emergency Committee explained what they'd concluded—I pounced. I wasn't going to let any other girl have him. So for that reason, I guess, I'm glad the Ring of Fire happened. And we did talk about it, when we first considered having kids. What it might be like for them as time went on."

"And I know that Dad's parents would have raised the roof if they were still alive. But they're not. They died way before the Ring of Fire and you can't let dead people run your life."

Carole finished up the nails. "Rose water and glycerin on your hands, please. Rub it in well." She stood up. As for Betty's hair... She sighed.

"What does Kristen think about all of this?

Kristen was the older daughter of Jerry Elias, Grantville's second dentist. The one who wasn't Henry Sims.

"Well..." Betty was just a couple of years older than Kristen. They hadn't been in the same class, but they'd been in the same school buildings most of the time they were growing up.

And, now, Kristen was married to Brad Laforrest.

"Well... She says that Brad has a bit of a hang-up about black identity."

Which was as far as Betty wanted to go.

What Kristen had actually said one evening, during a general "girls' night out and blowing off steam" session, was: "Why did I marry him? Well, call me shallow, but I wanted a husband with a college degree and a professional job and there weren't all that many of those running around Grantville unattached after the Ring of Fire happened. Brad has his B.S. Okay, it's in physical education rather than astrophysics, but there's no point in a girl's asking for the moon. He was working on an M.Ed.

"Call me even shallower, but I didn't want to marry a down-timer. Yeah, I know that quite a few women have, and I suppose that's okay if you don't actually want to ever talk to the person you marry. I wanted a husband, not some kind of a"—she paused to think—"not some kind of a social work project. I sure didn't want a life in which I'd always have to be thinking what word I needed to use when I reminded the guy I married that he needed to take out the garbage.

"So I'm not a pioneering spirit. I don't want to go out into the world and bring enlightenment to the masses. I'm hanging on by my fingernails right here, okay? Teaching seventh- and eighth-grade English at the middle school, picking up some of the girls' PE classes on top of that, plus tutoring English for GED students—I'm surviving one day at a time. And if that's not okay with you, you can like it or lump it.

"We both have steady jobs, we have two kids, and I hope we have more kids. Under the circumstances, that's about as good as it's going to get. I don't delude myself that it's valentines and roses on his side, either. He'd 'druther' have married a black woman if there was a 'druther' to be had. But the only young black woman who got caught in the Ring was Sharon Nichols, and she didn't have the slightest interest in him. And I don't think he considered going on an expedition to West Africa to find a wife."

Then Kristen had grinned. "But I'm just as glad that the Anti-Slavery Society expedition is leaving him behind in Grantville on the grounds that he's too tied down with a wife and kids to be sailing off on a ship for a year or two. Who knows what he'd decide to do if he got there and had an option."

* * *

Nissa Pritchard was getting tired of the whole thing. "I talked to Howard Selden—he's in the assisted living center, now; used to be the gate guard at the power plant," she exploded to Joanie and Lacy. "I doubt either of you ever met him. He doesn't know the Mundells, but he's seen them around town, of course. He says that no way is Lorrie Mundell a black woman.

"Why should we give a damn what James and Sharon Nichols might think? Even if Dr. Nichols and Sharon were still around Grantville, what would they know? They were here from out of town, for Rita's wedding. I doubt they've even met Lorrie."

"I talked to Carole again," Joanie said. "And then we managed to talk to Hal for a while in his copious spare time. This all goes a long time back, like, way, way, back. Lorrie's grandfather, August Dexter, was a thoroughly respectable white man; a Baptist preacher.

"August Dexter's sister was Berea Harris. She's been dead for nearly twenty-five years, but her husband, Henry Harris, lived until just a couple of years ago. He died right here in Grantville, after the Ring of Fire, in the Assisted Living Center. They had two kids of their own, and then no more. The boy, Dex Harris, died here in Grantville, less than a year ago."

She took a deep breath. "And the girl, Berea's daughter, married Horace Underwood and was Quentin's mother. Quentin Underwood who was killed at the oil field up north, at Wietze, in the French raid. Quentin's daughter Laura is named for her—for Berea's daughter."

"Random thought: was she named for that college?"

"No, they were both named for the place in the Bible, I think. Anyway, when August's wife Carrie died, Berea agreed to take in his two little boys. And was sort of surprised to find out that Carrie's brother's little girl—that was Glory Lou—got sent on the train from Kentucky as part of the package.

"Hal said that Glory Lou didn't 'pass for white,' exactly, any more than the Dexter boys did. It was just that Berea never saw any reason to say anything about their family background and they were all three light-skinned enough that nobody ever said anything. But the Harris family were bound to know, for sure, and the Underwoods would have, too."

When the questions got as far as Magdeburg, the only thing that Quentin's widow, Hope Underwood, said was: "Nobody in Grantville except the Harris and Underwood families had the slightest inkling, and I have *no idea* how it came up now. I'm sure I don't know how such gossip got started. I sure would never have mentioned it, and neither would Quentin. Everybody else who knew is dead." She took a deep breath. "Well, as far as I'm concerned, 'least said, soonest mended.' I hope it dies down."

* * *

Attacus Williams made his bathroom available for their "home barbershop" sessions, simply because it was the biggest bathroom. Likely, at some point in the past, it had been remodeled from a bedroom. Nobody knew for sure, since Grantville hadn't been the county seat and all the land records and building permits and such had stayed up-time in Fairmont.

"Walt Jenkins just can't cut black hair. I mean, he's willing to try, but he can't." Isaiah Avery contemplated the first time he'd been in a hurry and gone to the barber shop in Grantville rather than driving over to Fairmont. "That day, I eventually told him to shave it all off, and I'd start over."

"You've both married white women," Attacus pointed out.

"Yes, but."

"It's...well." Bradley said. "The first time I saw Kristen was in a faculty meeting. She was sitting two rows ahead of me, and I was looking at the back of her head. That trim, curly, black hair, cut close to her neck. And then she turned around to say something to someone behind me, and her eyes were black, too. And I thought..."

"You thought?"

"Yeah. I thought, *if I marry that woman, at least my kids won't come out looking as peculiar as O.J. Simpson's did.*"

"All of us married white women."

"You didn't."

"Actually, I think I'd classify a Rom woman as more white than black. Sort of like Middle Easterners."

"Are the Rom actually Middle Eastern?"

"I don't think anyone knows. Not for sure. Some of the legends say that they started out in India, maybe."

"That's a whole different ball game."

"So would you be so—uptight, I guess—about it all if that picture on Lorrie Mundell's wall had been of a Korean guy? Instead of a real light-skinned black man?"

"How would a Korean have gotten to Kentucky in the nineteenth century?"

"Missionaries. Those guys got around."

Which led to Joanie Smith getting real frazzled at the next meeting of the Anti-Slavery League. "What do you mean, 'What did I do about his hair?' You've never even seen Jason, have you? He joined the army right away after the Ring of Fire. What I did about his hair was cut it with my home barber set, just like I did Hank's. Still do cut Hank's. And my own. And Jessica's. In my opinion, it's too expensive for a whole family to pay the prices that barbers charge these days. Or it was for us, before the Ring of Fire. Jason has hair; it isn't anything special; just plain hair."

Lacy Brumfield understood the issue a little better. "What did I do about Tom's hair? Actually, Rick took him to Fairmont, to a barber there, once he got old enough to care. All Walt Jenkins ever managed to do was buzz it short with the electric clippers, which was fine when he was ten, but embarrassing when he was fifteen. And after he got his driver's license, he went on his own. It was no big deal."

Which bothered Brad Laforrest quite a bit. "But what do those two guys themselves feel about it? We're hearing from their adoptive mothers, not from them. Maybe they..."

Isaiah looked up from the papers he was shuffling in the guidance office. "I have bad news for you, Bradley my boy. Listen to me and pay attention—your undergraduate degree was in physical education. Mine was in psychology, and I've done a lot of looking and reading on this. No matter what they may look like, a kid who is brought up by a white woman is white. More if it's the mother than the dad, actually. The way he walks, the way he talks, the way he thinks about the world.

"If you want your kids to think they're black as they grow up, you're going to have a pretty steep hill to climb. That's what the association of black social workers were thinking about in the 1970s when they started fighting the practice of having biracial kids like the Smith and Brumfield boys adopted by white couples. The social workers said they ended up with 'racial identity' problems. Which is true, I suppose, if you're convinced that their racial identity has to be black. You're about as black as people come. Your main function on the WVU football team, until your injury, was to appear as a 'Great Big Black Bruiser of a football player.' I'm about as black as people come anywhere outside of central Africa, but I always came in more on the 'middle-sized, mild-mannered, Oreo of a nerd' location on the spectrum.

"But if you ask me, to quote Elvis, 'all shook up' is an identity, too."

"Well..." Brad leaned against the desk. "I can't say that I like it, but I guess I'll have to accept that Jason and Tom will be...well...whatever they are. But what about Lorrie Mundell? That woman is passing. That photo family tree she has up in her hallway..."

Joanie Smith wasn't happy when he said the same thing to her. "What the hell business is it of yours?"

"People shouldn't pretend to be what they aren't. That's dishonest. It would be one thing if she openly admitted that she was biracial, the way your kid does..."

"Dammit, Bradley, Lorrie isn't 'passing.' As I understand it, that involves hiding who you 'really' are and what your family was. If Lorrie Mundell was 'passing,' she wouldn't have had that picture up on her wall for you to see in the first place. The Mundells are sociable people. Friendly. They have committee meetings for this and that at their house, stuff to do with the school while the boys were growing up, friends. Several dozen people have to have walked up and down that hall, past that photo, over the years. I must have passed it twenty times, myself. I never noticed anything."

* * *

"Roberta, now they want to know if you can't look it all up somewhere."

"Up-time, I could have. I could have taken a research day, gone to the state historical society, and looked it up on microfilm. Or to the FHS at the bigger LDS church over in Fairmont, though I'd have had to order them there and wait for a couple of weeks for the reels to come in. But there just weren't copies of Kentucky census records in Grantville. I can't get them by waving my magic wand or pulling a rabbit out of a hat the way George Mundell did when he entertained at children's parties. It ain't gonna happen, and that's that. The best I can do now is ask Lorrie herself."

So, along with Sandra Prickett, also from the Genealogy Society, she did.

Lorrie tucked one leg up under her. The red vinyl kitchen chairs weren't really very comfortable to sit on.

"We're really Kentuckians, not from right around here, even if both Dad and Ma did grow up in Marion County, not very far from Grantville. Ma was working her way through Berea College when the family pushed her to marry Dad, on the grounds that he needed someone to keep him on the 'strait and narrow path.' I do mean family: they were first cousins on the Sams side. You can see that on the family tree."

"After he died—well, to be honest, he killed himself in a one-car DUI accident, whether he meant to or not—Ma went back to college and became a social worker. She stayed in Kentucky, never remarried, no other kids, was just about to retire when the Ring of Fire hit. I worry about how she's been making it, back up-time, with no one to look out for her."

"Didn't she have any other family?"

"She was an only child, too. Her mom died when she was born. That was in 1936, in the middle of the Depression, and they couldn't afford a doctor. Grandpa Sams remarried but didn't have any more kids. He and Pansy have both been dead for years. On the Dexter side, Jim, my dad, had a brother, my uncle Dave, but he was five or six years older than Ma. It's more likely that she would have to look after him than the other way around."

"August Dexter, the only one of them from around here—well, August was born in Kentucky, already, but his parents went through West Virginia—was a white man. He married Carrie Sams in Kentucky. Maybe the law said he shouldn't, but he did. Which probably means that when they went to the courthouse out there for a license, nobody noticed that Carrie wasn't white."

* * *

"So," Roberta said, "Carrie and Jerry's mother was named Geraldine Russell. She was Kentuckian and Lorrie's not sure about her family. But you saw her picture on the wall for yourself, Bradley. The only one of all of them that caused you a second look was Freeman Sams himself. One great-grandparent who died more than forty years before Lorrie was born. Well, because of the cousin-marriage thing, he shows up twice on the family tree, but even so."

Nissa Pritchard chimed in. "If you ask me, there's no way that Lorrie Mundell is a black woman passing as white. She's a white woman with a little bit of black somewhere in her family tree."

"How can you say that?"

"I can say it because being black has affected me every single day of my life. Where I lived, what jobs I got, how people treated me once I got on the job. Even now, after the Ring of Fire, living with Claude Yardley, who's white, in case you hadn't noticed. So I make the most of it, a lot of days. Put on the accent, put on the drawl. There are days when I can do a Disney stereotype with the best of them. Swing these hips and put on the attitude. That's what it means to be black. Having that man on her family tree hasn't affected Lorrie one single day of her life—not until you came along, Brad. Except maybe a couple when she went to the archives and tried to look him up, which wasn't exactly a big deal. So I say that she's not black. And not 'passing,' either. Roberta's going to talk to her some more."

* * *

"I did go to the archives and try to look them up, once, back when I was making that photo family tree that has Brad Laforrest so upset, but I didn't get very far. Let me show you." Lorrie opened the door to a cubbyhole under the stairs. There was a filing cabinet. Burnt orange color, maybe half as deep as most.

"That's a cute cabinet," Sandy Prickett said.

"Yeah, I know that I could sell it for something. But I'm using it. One of the boys can sell it after I'm gone." Lorrie riffled through the second drawer and pulled out a folder. "I made some copies off the microfilm. I suppose you would say that Freeman Sams was a very light-skinned 'man of color' as it was put at the time—at least by people who were trying to be polite. There were a lot of ruder words available. He was born in 1881, so he missed the 1880 census. The lady in charge said that the 1890 census burned. So here he is in 1900 in some absolutely unconnected family. Labeled 'boarder.'

"He graduated from Berea College—it was almost the only integrated college in the country back then—and worked as a railroad conductor, one of the few decent jobs open to him at the time, until he was killed in a union riot a few years before World War I.

"Here's his wife, Geraldine Russell, in the same census. She's a 'hired girl.' What was I supposed to do with that? From the picture—they're not together, it must have been taken at least twenty years after the one I have of him—she was even lighter-skinned, if she wasn't white. She was a domestic servant before her marriage. She didn't have the kind of schooling that he did.

"Freeman and Geraldine were both over 21 when they got married in 1907, so nobody signed permission slips for them. They had Carrie and Jerry, then Freeman died. So I gave up.

"After he was killed, she became a hotel housekeeper until she died and pushed her two kids to 'get educated like your father.' Which Carrie did, and Jerry didn't. Carrie attended Berea, became an elementary school teacher, and married a white man, August Dexter."

Roberta looked at the photocopies. "Did you look for other Sams and Russell families in that county in 1880? In 1900?"

Lorrie gave Roberta a blank look. "No. Why would I?"

In a world designed by Roberta Sutter, every high school student would take a required course in genealogical research methodology.

Unfortunately, somebody else had designed the world.

* * *

Mildred Baumgardner, at her dining room table, took the cover off her old manual typewriter, pulled out a sheet of paper, and started to copy another missive based on the publications of the American Tract Society for mailing to Lorrie Mundell.

Mildred had never liked George Mundell's wife. For that matter, she hadn't approved of George and his showing up in clown costumes at children's birthday parties, which was not a proper job. Even if he had a day job and only did that part-time.

She entirely agreed that movies—most of them, at least—were sinful, though Charlton Heston had made a fine-looking Moses in his day. From what she had read about such things as *Jesus Christ, Superstar!* though... Yes, most drama was likely sinful and blasphemous.

Albert Underwood was right about the Reverend Green, but at least the Green boy had been on the right side of the debate. A fine young man, who had never caused his parents a speck of trouble.

Which was more than she could say about her own grandchildren, unfortunately. Ronnie—marrying one of those Collins girls. Garrett—taking off with the army instead of staying home to assist his poor grandmother. Carly—moving out of the home that Mildred had provided to live with her good-for-nothing father on the estate of that trouble-making heretical countess!

Leaving her here in the house with—April! Who wasn't even hers by blood! One of Tina's by her first husband. April—if April wasn't here, doing all the chores and upkeep—and, to be honest, most of the work of making sure the boarders living in the now-extra rooms kept things clean and orderly—she'd have to go back to the Bowers Assisted Living Center, which she had hated.

Mildred was a hunt-and-peck typist, but she was persistent.

Alas! the theater does not properly instruct a man how to live, how to suffer, how to die. It does not tend to inspire those serious, practical sentiments which befit one who remembers that he may be called tomorrow to leave this transient scene. On the contrary, its direct and only tendency is, to make men forget their duty and their real happiness, and altogether to beguile the feelings proper for one who has no continuing city here, but who ought to be continually seeking one to come, whose builder and maker is God.

Augustine of Hippo lived on, even if Mildred Baumgardner had never heard of him. Much less of Plato.

* * *

There was another meeting of the Anti-Slavery League. Another loss of focus.

Nissa Pritchard had the floor. "Brad, I wish that you would just leave it alone. Lorrie's not the result of some slave-owner raping a slave. Well, maybe somewhere, way back when, since the Sams family was already light-skinned, but not in her memory. Or her parents' memories. Or even her grandparents' memories. I talked to Roberta Sutter at the genealogical society about it. She talked to Lorrie herself. She's not pretending to be anything. It is what it is."

"You went to the play, didn't you?" Joanie asked. "*The Importance of Being Earnest*?"

"Yeah, Kristen wanted to see it."

"You saw Lorrie on stage, being an English aristocrat?"

"Yeah."

"Did your eyes and ears tell you, 'There's a black American twentieth-century woman up there pretending to be an English aristocrat?"

"No. She was all the way into the eighteenth-century thing. Nineteenth century? When was it set?"

"So who cares, really? The point is... On the stage, she was Lady Bracknell. Here in Grantville, she's Lorrie Mundell. Leave it at that."

"Look, Brad," Attacus Williams said. "Pull your mind out of damned antebellum Dixie with all the hooped skirts and look at history. There were plenty of cultures in Africa run by black people who had slaves, black people who captured other black people and sold them as slaves. Just like, if you go to the movies, there were plenty of cultures in Europe run by white people who had slaves who were white. I found that out the first time when they showed *Quo Vadis* in Sunday School when I was a kid. Not on Sunday morning; youth group on Thursday evenings. Greeks. Romans. That came up in Western Civ my freshman year. I'm a City Colleges of Chicago guy, even worked there as an IT tech for a few years, back when Nelvia Brady was the chancellor. Chinese people had Chinese slaves. Probably, if there are aliens out in space, they have alien slaves. We can sit here in a meeting of the Anti-Slavery League and be as high-minded as we like, but the only thing that's going to get rid of slavery, probably, in the long run, is industrialization. Until some busybody decides that computers and robots have souls!"

Attacus, unlike the school-based group, had come to Grantville as a construction worker for the fiber optics plant and now was an employee of Grantville-Saalfeld Foundries and Metalworks. And something of a missionary for modernization.

Grantville, SoTF
May 1637

"...another page of those anti-drama tracts," Melissa Higginbottom said.

"That's disgusting," Renee Carson said. "Let's hope that Mr. Marmion ignores this one. Or Mrs. Mundell doesn't tell him about it. It's not as if neo-Puritans are the only retrograde people around. Colleen, my dad's wife—you know her, she's the veterinarian's sister—invited me over there for dinner last Sunday. Command performance, in dramatic terms. She was saying that as long as there are plenty of nannies, there's no reason she shouldn't go on pumping out babies as fast as God wants to give them to her, because otherwise we'll run out of up-timers pretty soon and pregnancy isn't that much of a nuisance. She's expecting again. This will be number four."

Renee looked toward the door of the high school drama room to see if Mr. Marmion was on his way in or if she had time for a little more gossip.

No teacher in sight.

"That was when *I* said that if the babies are brought up by down-time nannies, they'll basically grow up to be down-timers, because just coming out of her magic hoo-ha won't turn them into twentieth-century Americans as they grow up."

Someone cleared his throat.

She twisted her neck and looked toward the back of the room.

Shackerley Marmion backed out of the supply closet. "What, precisely, is a magic hoo-ha? Not that I fail to grasp the general concept from context, you understand."

Renee swallowed.

Amalia Hartmann laughed out loud.

Laura Cunningham answered with the precision ingrained in her by a mother who helped manage the Grantville Research Center. "In a lot of romance novels, the hero was a hopeless rake, womanizing all over the map, hopping from one bed to another, never staying the night. Then he met the heroine, who suddenly turned him into a model of gentlemanly fidelity. Because she had a magic hoo-ha, you understand." She grinned like an imp.

"Mr. Marmion!" Renee squeaked. ""Don't you *dare* write one of your bawdy plays about my stepmother's magic hoo-ha. At least, not until I've graduated and gone off to college somewhere. Which won't be the technical college here in Grantville, believe you me, considering that Dad's on the faculty! Not that I didn't point out to Colleen that Dad doesn't have the best track record when it comes to staying with his wives and she could pump a half dozen infants and then find herself bringing them up on her own and not able to afford the nannies."

"Perhaps," Marmion said, "the class should come to order."

* * *

In the event, all that Marmion said this time was that the most recent broadside contained no more than a repeat of the diatribe against representing oneself to be other than what one was created to be. The author of the tract was making an extended statement, so to speak, on the old proverb: *She is nother fyshe nor fleshe, nor good red hearyng.*

The in-class conversation kept going at lunch.

"According to Aunt Tammy," Melissa Higgenbottom said as she plopped her tray down, "Heidi Davis up in Erfurt is saying pretty much the same thing as Colleen. She only had two kids before the Ring of Fire and that's all she wanted, but now she's going to have as many as she can produce."

"Be fair," Laura said. "The first baby Heidi had after the Ring died as a toddler. That's enough to push any woman a bit off kilter. Plus, Heidi's an only child and her parents were left up-time. She's a Bozarth, but she's not all that close kin to the rest of the Bozarths here in town."

"Not true," Melissa said. "Brick's her uncle; Roberta and Maurine are her aunts."

"Brick's been off in Regensburg for years," Laura countered, "and he took his family. Roberta's in the Bowers Assisted Living Center because of rheumatoid arthritis. Two of her kids were left up-time and Dina Mer-rifield is off in the wilds doing geology."

Melissa shook her head. "But Maurine and Gordon are in Erfurt, so Heidi has them. And Gena's there. She married Eric Hudson last year, so Heidi has an aunt and an uncle and a cousin up there. Gordon Kroll knows Uncle Bill pretty well. He's the one who told Uncle Bill about what Heidi says she's going to do and Uncle Bill told Aunt Tammy. Gordon thinks that Heidi's off her rocker. And guys say that women gossip!"

"What does it sound like we're doing?" Natasha Clinter asked.

"Oh, Tash," Renee said. "You're just so...naturally well-behaved. I can't believe that you even sit at the same table with the rest of us."

"Mr. Clinter probably tells Tash to do it." Melissa pouted. "We're her charity cases. The good girl making a statement that the weird ones shouldn't be treated like outcasts. Left to herself, she'd probably sit with the other good girls like Alicia Rice and Nona Dobbs."

Tash blushed. "I...I'm not naturally well-behaved. I just pretend to be. I don't want to disappoint Dad and Mom, the way Carson did, by dropping out of school and turning into a barista at Sternbock's."

"What you are," Renee said, "is over-sensitive about being adopted. And I can tell you, because I'm a Carson by birth, with all that means for getting to eavesdrop when the grown-ups think I'm doing something else...." She stopped and looked around. Nobody was too close to their table. "You know that the self-righteous like Nina don't talk about it, but Dad's cousin Vanna had Lissa three years before she married Okey Rush?"

Tash nodded.

"Well, six years before that, she had Carson, and it's not as if she shouldn't have known better. She was thirty years old. Of course, she didn't get her nursing degree until after the Ring of Fire, so maybe she didn't understand about biology. Nina claims that Vanna always had a taste for low-lifes with muscles when it came to men, which is why she worked at a gym in Fairmont. She arranged a private adoption for him with your parents, who wanted a boy, but that's why his first name is Carson. You can blame his sulks and dropping out of school on his general Carson-ness. So there."

Tash blinked. "Then why did they get me a couple of years later? They already had two grown-up girls. They might have wanted a boy when they adopted Carson, but they didn't need another daughter."

"They're glad they have you now, since the other two got left up-time," Melissa Higgenbottom answered. "Just count your blessings."

"Okey Rush isn't a low-life; he's a professor at Jena," Laura Cunningham protested.

Renee looked around again. "He probably isn't Lissa's biological father, either. And don't repeat me on that. A lot of the down-timers are harder on kids born out of wedlock than even Albert Underwood and Nina are. Anyway, he was just an ordinary county government grunt taking classes for his M.A. when he married Vanna. Not a prominent professor at an eminent university."

It was probably just as well that the bell rang, because Laura was on the verge of pointing out that Okey Rush didn't have muscles—more of a paunch, but maybe he'd been in better shape when Vanna married him, because that was a dozen years ago.

Melissa had a follow up to "glad they have you now" right on the tip of her tongue.

Tash had been about to ask, "Do you know where they got me? Do you know who I really am?"

Sometimes, she felt like she had gone through her entire life pretending to be someone that she wasn't.

Renee had been about to proclaim, "If I ever get out of this damned town, I'm not coming back. Ever. I don't blame Michelle a bit for staying in Amberg for the last two years, even if there were Bavarian armies stomping all over the Upper Palatinate for a while."

Shortly thereafter, the girls had a wonderful idea.

"*Kiss Me Kate*?" Mr. Marmion said. "I am not familiar with the title."

"You'll know it as *The Taming of the Shrew*," Laura answered. "*The Taming of the Shrew* with music. It's just the thing to lure Massinger's Men back."

"Because, really, you know," Renee said, "Grantville just isn't the same without them. They ought to be here. At least for part of the year! They've got to be bored to death in dear old Butzbach. When it comes to progressive culture, Grantville is where it's at!"

* * *

Lorrie had been pushed too far and was ready to push back. But she didn't want to argue with Brad Laforrest any place public, like the school. Or drop in at his and Kristen's house.

"I don't," she told Joanie, "really know them that well."

So Carole got Betty to haul them over to the salon after work one day. Amid the bottles and the scents and everything that went with a beauty parlor.

"You were a guest in my home," Lorrie said. "After you saw the photos, if you had wanted to know, if you were curious, you could have just asked me. I'd have told you. I told Roberta and Sandy when they came and asked me, after you started stirring up such a fuss.

"I want to know something, since you're so upset because you think that I'm 'passing.' What are you suggesting, Brad? What do you think would be fair? That I should walk around every day of my life, everywhere I go, wearing a sandwich board that says, 'Not every single one of my ancestors was white.' Nobody's going to notice it, otherwise. You said yourself that you'd seen me around town a lot and it never even occurred to you. And I know you asked other people, other black people, who told you the same thing.

"So what do you think I should be doing, then? Do you want to design an emblem for me? Sort of like the yellow star of David that the Nazis made the Jews wear? Isn't that what the whole *Krystalnacht* was against? You're as damnably 'racist in reverse' as any southern Jim Crow politician who pushed the 'one drop theory.' Fuck your whole identity crisis.

"Fuck you and the horse you rode in on."

June 1637

Shortly after Massinger's Men got back from Butzbach, earlier than they were expected, they set to staging a number of the new plays that Master Massinger and Tom Quiney had written while they were out of Grantville. Along with Massinger's "English alternate history" sequence, everyone pretty much agreed that the two "Engaine" plays, based on Thomas B. Costain's *The Black Rose*, were the best things he had ever written.

Lorrie's acting ability really wasn't up to the ambitious countess of Bulaire (Massinger had dropped the "earl of Lessford" title for Rauf of Bulaire, oppressive, evil, Norman overlord that he was, as unnecessarily confusing to the audience).

"No more," she said, "it would have been up to Lady Macbeth if I'd ever been silly enough to try it, and I know it. Using connivance to trap a nobleman into marriage, viciously ordering six commoners to be hanged from trees—no, just not my style." She was happy to take the minor role of Lady Tressling, Engaine's mother, feckless spouse of a mean drunk.

Nonetheless, since "her boys" were now partners in the company, during the curtain calls at the end of *The Tragedy of Engaine of Bulaire, Part 1*, Massinger once again swept her a deep bow and once more declared, "Mistress Mundell, thou art passing fair."

* * *

The three excepts from a tract are from:

The Christian and the Theater. Published by the American Tract Society.

https://www.gracegems.org/ATS/theater.htm

The genealogy article mentioned by a character is:

Carter, Kent. "Wantabes and Outalucks: Searching for Indian Ancestors in Federal Records." Ancestry Newsletter 5, no. 6 (November-December 1987): 1-6.

From Cramps To Matrimony
Terry Howard

The Holiday Lodge, just outside the Ring Wall,

Grantville

Spring 1636

"Room service, my wife is having cramps, and she requires a cup of Raspberry Mint tea. And I'd like a cup of Green Apple tea." The telephone, with its horn cup to one's ear and another cup on the short pole that you spoke into, was just one of the many modern wonders offered by the Holiday Lodge.

"I'm sorry, sir, but neither is on the menu. We have Chamomile tea. Should I send for the attending physician?"

"No, we don't need a physician. We need a cup of Raspberry Mint tea. And don't be ridiculous. This is Grantville. It's where McAdams Raspberry Mint tea comes from. Our physician prescribed Raspberry Mint tea to my wife for cramps when we were here last year. My wife is cramping, and it's the only thing that is going to calm them for her. We only brought a small amount with us because we were coming to Grantville. This is a luxury hotel. McAdams Raspberry Mint tea and Green Apple tea are luxuries. Do something about it. Send up a teapot of hot water, and we'll steep our own for today. But I will expect you to have it on hand for tomorrow. This is Grantville, after all."

When the hot water arrived, Aaron Bodner steeped a cup of Raspberry Mint tea for his wife and a cup of Green Apple tea for himself. The couple sat in comfortable chairs in front of the suite's fireplace, and Lord Bodner watched his wife's face calm as the tea eased her cramps. He made a mental note to call down in the morning and confirm that the lodge had made arrangements to get the tea. What point was there in staying in a luxury hotel if they could not get you what you wanted? If they did not have those teas, then, after he took his wife to see the doctor, they would move to the Higgins Hotel and he would go get the tea she needed from the pharmacy at the hospital. He just hoped that the doctor would not start talking about a hysterectomy. His wife still very much wanted to have children.

Sarah, the assistant kitchen manager, looked over the note from the front desk and called the McAdams Mining Company.

Ludwig's mother answered the kitchen phone. "McAdams Mining Company. Madde speaking. How may we help you?"

When the four boys finally had a phone line turned on to the house their three families shared, they put it in the kitchen and listed it in the company's name. Ludwig's mother took orders and messages, giving her what she had been wanting, a job beyond cooking and childcare. The families used the phone and gave out the number. But anyone calling got a business line. So, they did not linger just to chat.

"This is Sarah at the Holiday Lodge. I need a pound of Raspberry Mint tea right away."

"Frau Sarah, we sell it in half-pint jars. If you want it by the pound, we can arrange it. But you are a regular customer, so I should tell you, if we go to Johnson's Grocery and get enough half-pint jars to make a pound for you it will cost you a lot more than if you send someone after the half-pint jars yourself."

"Johnson's Grocery has McAdams Raspberry Mint tea?"

"Johnson's has Mountain Top Teas. They are the same teas which become McAdams Teas when those people up there"—the questionable acceptance of Anabaptists showed up in the disapproving word choice and tone of voice—"put the boys' labels on the jars."

"So, if you have it, Johnson's has it?"

"Johnson's Grocery has four Mountain Top Teas they carry in bulk. You can get Raspberry Mint tea from the pharmacy at the hospital. We supply a variety of twelve teas in half-pint jars. Which Johnson's Grocery carries on their shelves."

"Well, when you send our weekly supply of blue cheese, send us a jar of each of the teas Johnson's does not have in bulk. We already stock the four teas Johnson sells in bulk. I'll have my people pick up the other eight varieties from Johnson's for now. I assume we can get the teas more cheaply from you."

"Certainly, Frau Sarah. Do you want a jar of each of our jams, jellies, and condiments? You might have a customer ask for one of them, and it wouldn't be a bad thing to have on hand." Ludwig's mother was an excellent sales agent.

"Sure, go ahead. It won't hurt to be prepared," Sarah answered.

* * *

When the kitchen manager went over the books at the end of the week, he called across the office, "Sarah, where in the world did you find that

A-Plus steak sauce Herr Doktor Schmitt was so disappointed that we did not have?"

"Did it come in with the rest of the McAdams Mining Company's inventory?" Sarah looked up from proofing the proposed menu for the coming week before it went to the printers. "I figured if we had one upset guest because we didn't have their favorite brand, it wouldn't hurt to stock the rest of the company's selection."

"Why didn't we think of them when the professor was here?" the manager asked.

"Why in the world is a mining company selling tea and steak sauce?" Sarah countered.

"It started out with them selling fresh mushrooms out of an empty coal mine. Then our night clerk moved his blue cheese operation into their mine and they started exporting blue cheese, then dried mushrooms, then ground coffee beans, then anything else that would sell. Apparently, A-Plus steak sauce is one of theirs. I should have thought of that at the time. Anyway, since they work out of a mine, they called themselves a mining company." The manager got the story mostly right.

"Look, order another bottle of the sauce and send it to Herr Doktor Schmitt at whatever university he's from with our compliments and assure him that, the next time he stays with us, we will have a supply on hand. Then keep two bottles on hand and order a new one when the first one gets opened, as we do with the rarer wines we keep in stock."

The chef in the kitchen opened and sampled everything Sarah had ordered. Those items he wanted, Sarah sent a messenger up the mountain to buy directly from the Baptist farm.

"I'll tell you the same thing we told the grocery stores when they wanted to start carrying the teas," came the reply. "We sell wholesale. That's bulk in gallon lots. If you want some of our jellies in smaller jars, talk to the

McAdams Mining Company. I'm sure they will put in an order for any size jar you want. But we fill the jars they provide, so if you want to buy gallons of something, we'll be happy to fill whatever jars or containers you provide to us. If you want it under your own label, send us the label layout, and we will print up the labels."

The Lodge settled, mostly, for buying half-pints through the mining company. But they bought a collection of one-quart jars with wire and glass lids and sent them up to the Mountain Top Baptist Bible Institute for mayonnaise because the farm's just tasted better. The chef, though he did try, could not match it. The same was true for their mustard. The secret was their dark wild honey. The chef could match their ketchup, barbeque sauce, and steak sauce, but why bother when it could be had at reasonable prices at need? He put in an order from the mining company and asked for individual serving jars. The glass blowers started a line of small, one-serving sample jars that hotel guests were taking home as mementos. The farm started getting larger jars and sample jars from the mining company along with the standard half-pint jars.

* * *

Doktor Adolph Schmitt of the Theology Department of the University of Rostock, in the province of Mecklenburg, opened the package and then read the note.

His colleague, Herr Doktor Georg Seeberger, with whom he shared an office, took note of the package when it arrived. It was clearly not of a size to be a book. "Whatever is it, Adolph?"

"When I stayed in Grantville, on one occasion, I dined in the hotel's dining room. It being Grantville, I asked for a sauce I'd had at Krimmer's which Frau Krimmer identified as being from Grantville. They did not have it. It seems they found a source and sent me a sample."

"They are a strange people, these Englishmen of Grantville."

"Oh, they speak a form of English all right. But remember to identify them as Americans after the New World. You will find that they are adamant about insisting on their New World identity."

"I've always wondered." Georg asked, "when you were in Grantville, did you get a chance to review their Doctor Green's famous library?"

"Yes, I did. I spent a morning perusing his library with only a student to assist me. Then I shared lunch with the doctor and his community of students and chatted with him and them in the afternoon. He spent the morning farming. I asked the student that morning if it was seemly that a doctor should be grubbing in the dirt."

"A valid question," Doktor Seeberger agreed.

"Well, the lad quoted the English heretic, John Ball. 'When Adam delved and Eve span, who was then the gentleman?' Then he told me that the priesthood of all believers required that all who would share in the bounty should likewise share in the work."

"I had heard that the people of Grantville took their republicanism seriously, but that is a bit extreme, don't you think? It is, as you said, unseemly. Does he deserve the title doctor if he is willing to so degrade himself?"

Adolph replied, "I was wondering that myself until I talked with him. He has a grasp of the Early Church Fathers that is truly incredible. There is not a classical work of the Fathers that he does not know well, and he has them all on his shelves, sometimes in two and three versions. He has works that we have assumed were lost, he has works we never dreamed existed. There is not one of the Fathers in Greek that he cannot discuss freely without referring to the printed page. His Latin is not as good, but it is adequate. And his grasp of the classical Greek philosophers is poor. He has little use for them."

"They say he is a heretic?" Seeberger asked.

"Without a doubt. He freely admits it without reservation. You could go so far as to say he glories in it. Even within his own heretical fellowship, he is not considered orthodox."

Georg looked surprised. "And they let him teach?"

"Well, for all that he is a heretic, he is a congenial fellow, easy to argue with and easy to like. He will strive valiantly to find some way of stating the proposition that will let all agree. And when he fails, he will smile and say, 'Well, then, we must agree to disagree. Let us set a date to discuss it again in heaven. Look for me in the shade of a tree of life on the banks of the river of life that flows from the throne of God. The one farthest from the throne. I'm sure we will not want to disturb God with our arguing when we hash it out after we have an eternal perspective."

"And he expects to be there?" Seeberger shook his head, yet it seemed an honest question.

"Well, yes, it would seem so. It is a common belief in Grantville. While I was there, I heard a most insulting story that illustrates their attitude."

"Oh?"

"Yes. The story goes that someone of note had died, and St. Peter met him at the pearly gates and gave him a tour while escorting him to his mansion. Early on, they passed the Baptists who were splashing and dunking each other in the river of life, while on the banks of the river, a choir of Fisher's Charismatics sang away in perfect harmony in some unknown tongue, and there was a park beyond the river full of narrow streets divided into small squares so there was an endless number of street corners with a Lollard, or a Socinian, or a Hussite——and who knows who else—four to an intersection preaching away and arguing away to their heart's content. As they approached a wall with three gates, Peter held his finger to his lips and said softly, 'Please be quiet when you pass this wall. Beyond,'—he pointed to each gate in turn—'are the Catholics, the Lutherans, and the Calvinists, and each of them thinks they are the only ones here.'"

Georg snorted. "I see what you mean. It is indeed insulting."

"Yet the person who told it to me thought it was quite hilarious. And it is Green's attitude, precisely, and moreover, it is Grantville's attitude also. The town collects heretics like a lodestone collects bits of iron. Almost every congregation they brought with them through time are heretics, and anyone at risk for his theology these days is fleeing there where they are welcomed and allowed, indeed encouraged, to prosper. There are multiple synagogues, of different groups and types of Jews. There is even an onion-domed Eastern Orthodox chapel funded by Russia. They now have two groups of up-time Baptists. And two groups of ordinary Anabaptists who somehow manage to share a building with worship space over a bar and grill, while arguing non-stop in the bar below where people come to watch and consider it entertainment. There is a third ordinary Anabaptist group who meet at the high school, Mennonites who mixed in with the up-time group who donated their building for the hospital in town. Plus, a group of atheists meet at the high school every Wednesday night to discuss their mutual damnation. It's Grantville's proud contention that everyone has the right to go to hell any way they please. Grantville's people value and guard their rights assiduously and will see to it that one and all are undisturbed in their pursuit of the fiery damnation of their choice. They are muchly concerned about an individual's rights, especially their right to vote. I was there for an election, and a herd of swine in an apple orchard after a windstorm could not have been more stirred up. More than one tavern set up a stage and encouraged debates leading up to that election and considered it entertainment.

"The Catholics brought St. Mary's with them, and they were also holding services at the high school during the initial refugee crisis. They built

St Elizabeth's near the fairgrounds. They didn't have a Lutheran church in town. There's a Lutheran renegade pastor in a storefront now and St. Martin's and St. Thomas's just outside of the Ring Wall on opposite sides of Grantville. Who was the Roman who complained that all that is vile is attracted to Rome? The same can be said of Grantville. And Green sits atop a mountain, overseeing it all with approval."

"And they let him teach?" Georg was still having trouble with the lack of control.

Adolph smiled at his colleague. "The mountaintop farm that supports the college is effectively his. It is not a matter that they let him teach. It is more a matter that he will let anybody study. But if you stay beyond guesting for a day or two, you will find that, on the third day, they will put you to work for half a day, and if you stay more than a week or so, they will want to discuss what you will be studying. It might not cost you anything, and they do eat well, but I would not say it was by any means free. So, if you don't care to grub in the dirt, milk cows, or collect eggs, then you make your selection of what you wish to study, buy copies of the books you want, and hope your selection is already in print, or you might have to wait a while."

Georg was all but wringing his hands and changed the topic. "So, the hotel in Grantville sent you a sauce?"

"The Holiday Lodge, yes. The sauce has a delightful flavor when added to grilled beef just before you eat it."

"I'll have my cook prepare grilled beef this Saturday. Bring your sauce and join us around six o'clock. I'm curious as to just why a sauce is that important."

* * *

After Saturday's dinner, Frau Seeberger sent a letter to Grantville, and in short order, not more than a month, a peddler showed up at her kitchen door.

"*Ich heisse* Hermann from McAdams Mining Company in Grantville."

"I am sorry," Anna the maid told him, "but, for something of this sort, Frau Seeberger would have to be consulted. She is indisposed today with a headache and I am not about to disturb her."

The peddler smiled. "Wait right here. Let me get you a free sample out of the cart." When he returned, he had three small paper packages. "This is aspirin. Give her two of these with a cup of willow bark and mint tea." Hermann lifted a second bag. "Put the tea leaves in a small container, add a cup of boiling water, cover it, and let it set for five minutes. Then strain the tea into a cup. The headache will be gone in half an hour. Give her two more aspirin and another cup of tea in the morning." He pointed at the third bag. "I shall stop back tomorrow before leaving town to see Frau Seeberger about the A-Plus sauce after which she inquired."

* * *

"What is this?" Frau Seeberger, sitting alone in the quiet and darkened room, demanded in an angry but soft voice.

"The A-Plus sauce peddler from Grantville said to take the two blue pills and drink the tea and the headache will be gone in half an hour." Anna quietly set the tray down as she quickly retreated.

* * *

The next day the peddler was back. "Did Frau Seeberger inquire after our A-Plus steak sauce?" Hermann took a jar from the sample carrier and set it on the table.

"I must have those blue pills and that wonderful tea," Frau Seeberger demanded.

"Certainly, madam." Hermann had a carpenter's tool carrier divided into squares to keep the half-pint jars from coming into contact with each other. He pulled out the aspirin and the mint tea. "Will one jar of tea suffice until I come through town again next month?"

* * *

In the office at the university the next day, Doktor Seeberger said, "Adolph, my wife sent for that sauce we so enjoyed. While the peddler was here, he sold her some pills and some tea. She has opened the drapes to the window in the sitting room for the first time in years, and she is reading again without complaint. Assure me again that there is no truth to the rumors of witchcraft in Grantville."

Doktor Schmitt snorted. "There is heresy aplenty. There are mechanical marvels to match; there are cocky braggarts in abundance who do not know how to respect a person of worth, and a modestly dressed woman is someone all but forgotten, or a visiting tourist. But no. There is no witchcraft. They do not need it. Why enchant a broom when your mechanics can make a flying machine? Why cast a spell when your physicians have pills? Why remove a mangled limb when your surgeons can repair it? Why make a deal with the devil when your fellow man can offer you a better one?"

"But the blue pills do seem to work magic," Seeberger said.

"Georg, if you are worried, go see Hendrik and get some matching pills that do nothing and swap them. Then watch and see. Didn't he tell you there was nothing wrong with your wife that a daily walk would not cure?"

"Yes, but she was sure otherwise."

"I suspect that the peddler said it would work, and her belief was all the magic it took. But the Chamomile tea is quite pleasant."

"She is drinking a mint tea," Georg replied.

"Oh, what I was served in Grantville was something called chamomile."

"I just wish the little jars didn't cost so much," Seeberger said.

"Are the empties accumulating in your kitchen or are the servants taking them to the pawnbroker? You should be able to recoup a portion of the cost by selling the empties. In Grantville, the manufacturer has a buy-back program."

"I'll have to look into that."

* * *

Doktor Seeberger entered the door under the three-balls sign of the pawnbroker on his way home from work. "Good day to you. Do you have any Grantville glass jars?'

"Not at the moment. I get about four a month. But they don't stay on the shelf long."

"So they sell well, then?"

"They do a very good job of keeping things dry," the broker said.

"Out of curiosity, what would you pay for a gross of them?"

"You know, I think I could sell a gross." The emphasis was clearly on the word *could*. "I think I can pay the same price apiece for a gross that I can pay for them one at a time. Do you have a gross?"

"I can get them—if it's worth the bother?"

The pawnbroker named a price.

"Let me see what I can do," Seeberger said.

When he got home, he told the cook, Greta, "Save the Grantville jars for me from now on. And when the McAdams peddler stops next time, send him to see me at the university."

* * *

"Herr Doktor Professor Seeberger, there is a tradesman at the door asking after you," Hans, a student receptionist, announced. Disapproval was clear in his voice.

"Yes, admit him, please."

The professor bought twelve dozen jars of varied sizes. When he asked after the price between empty and full, he bought them full with the mumbled comment, "I can empty them before I sell them." He smiled at the thoughts of what he would make selling the empty ones to the pawnbroker and at the luxuries he would enjoy at a lower cost.

* * *

"Master Seeberger?" Greta the cook approached the professor as he read in the front room one evening, not long after his jars had arrived.

"Yes?"

"Is it correct that we are selling the dried mushrooms for the same price the peddler was getting?"

"What?"

"I had someone stop by the kitchen door asking after dried mushrooms. The peddler stopped and told her that you had the full line of McAdams' products, and she should buy from you because he wouldn't be selling retail in town anymore. The buyer said she complained to the peddler that you would want too much, and the peddler shrugged and said you bought wholesale so you could afford to keep the same retail prices or close to it. I sold her a jar to get rid of her. What am I supposed to do?"

"Let me go back to my office. I have a list of what he was getting retail. And yes, with the discount he gave me for wholesale, we can turn a small profit selling retail. Since we aren't selling anything that is made locally, there shouldn't be a problem."

* * *

After a few weeks, Augustus Muller, the mayor's nephew and an assistant to the town council, showed up at the Seeberger home one evening.

"Herr Doktor Professor Seeberger, are you aware that someone is running an import business out of your kitchen?"

"I wouldn't say we are running a business. I bought some things in quantity because it was cheaper. The peddler's regular customers have been picking up what they want here since the peddler is no longer making his rounds."

"And he is no longer paying the import fees."

"None of what I bought is made locally. There is no competition to discourage. So there should be no import fees."

"You are running a business, so you are going to have to open a booth in the market."

"But I'm not interested in running a market booth. I'd have to have a booth built and hire someone to run it."

"You've been running a business out of your kitchen. Rent the booth space and pay the fees. My cousin," Augustus said, "has a booth you can buy at a very good price. It's a little run down, but you can have it painted."

"But I am not doing that much business. I'll put a stop to it."

"It has come to the council's attention. Open a booth on market days or be fined."

"Fined?"

The functionary named a sum, and the professor paled.

"Well, it will be cheaper to pay the fine."

"But since you have been selling things out of your kitchen you will be paying the booth space and the fees anyway for the last three months!"

"What?"

"Open the booth and accept forgiveness or pay the fine and fees for the last three months. Then, a month from now, you can close down and admit that you should leave marketing to the professionals."

"I see. I am to be a lesson. Who is it that has the booth they want to sell?" Professor Seeberger was sure in his heart that buying the booth was what this was really all about anyway.

* * *

Unbeknownst to everyone except the cook and the carriage driver, Hannah, the cook's niece, had been sleeping in the hayloft of the Seeberger's carriage house since her father died and she had a falling-out with her stepmother. She was very happy to run the booth on market days for a modest commission.

"You have raised your prices!" The shopper who had been buying at the kitchen door complained.

"A bit," Hannah admitted. "But the city council insists that we must have a booth, so they must pay me to sit here all day. If you are unhappy, tell your councilor to let us go back to selling out of the kitchen."

"Well, I don't like it, but I must have the blue cheese and the mushrooms."

And again, another customer said, "This is highway robbery."

Hannah shrugged, "The city council has decreed that—"

"Yes, I understand, but if we run out of the little blue pills, the mistress will fire the lot of us. So, we have no choice but to pay your exorbitant prices."

And again, "Thank goodness, you have the Raspberry Mint tea. Make sure you have more of it next month. We've found nothing else that will ease Frau Seeberger's cramps like the Raspberry Mint tea. Our lives are unbearable when the mistress is cramping."

* * *

"Auntie," Hannah handed Greta a list. "How soon can you get more of these?"

"When the peddler comes around—but Professor Seeberger will not want them. He regrets that he ever bought in quantity. He wants to get out as soon as the council will let him."

"But he mustn't! I will have my dowry saved up in just six months! The buyers are expecting the things that I'm out of. We are the most expensive booth in the market, and while I am not the busiest, I am busy. People are watching, and now they are asking what it is that I am selling that others are willing to pay such a high price for. People want the jars. I can't keep the empty ones in the booth. People buy things to get the jars. The ones who bought out of the kitchen door say they simply must have more of what they want. So, the people who bought the tea or the jam or whatever to get a jar to keep something dry are going to want more tea. I raised the prices to keep something on the shelf and people are still buying."

"Show me the account book." Greta perused the ledger. "Hmm? I will speak to the professor."

* * *

When Hermann the peddler came to the kitchen door at the end of the month, before he could say a word, Greta told him, "You must go to the university and speak to Professor Seeberger."

At the university, before Professor Seeberger got past a rather cold greeting, the peddler handed him a half-pint jar full of little wooden sticks.

"What are these?"

The label on the half-pint jar read, "McAdams Mining Co." in small letters at the top of the label. Under that in larger letters it read, "Grantville Matches."

Professor Adolph Schmitt, who shared his office space, was studiously not noticing that his colleague was interacting with a tradesman.

The peddler smiled and took a stick out of his hat band and scratched it across a rough surface. A flame sprouted on the end of the match. Then he blew it out. "I'll give you a free jar so you can let people try them out. I want you to buy a gross of them. If you've got more than half of them left next month when I come through again, I'll buy them back."

"But I..."

Seeberger was going to say he wanted out. But the cook's niece didn't want out. The booth was more than breaking even, even with the extra expenses. He could carry the cost of amortization on the start-up for the booth. It was plain to see that these 'matchsticks' were going to sell well.

"I'll take a gross of your matches. Stop back to the house and fill the list the cook has. She has the money to pay you."

When the peddler was gone, Adolph Schmitt spoke somewhat disapprovingly. "I thought you were resolved to get out of business."

"Adolph, I'm not selling things personally. I'm just financing my cook's niece. The poor girl just lost her father and needs a job."

Adolph snorted.

"Hey, the new imperial law says that nobles can be in business without losing status," Seeberger said.

Adolph snorted again.

Georg opened the jar and handed the man a matchstick. "Scratch something."

His colleague looked at him. "Go ahead, scratch something. No, scratch the colored end."

It burst into flame. Schmitt yelped and dropped it and then stamped it out.

"What kind of evil black magic was that?" he demanded.

"They're from Grantville and I have it on the finest authority that there is no witchcraft in Grantville. With these you don't have to keep a flame burning or strike a spark and nurse the tinder to start a fire. They are going to sell very well. My cook's niece is going to make a lot of money, and she will pay back what I thought I had lost through my foolishness. I will have a happy cook. She makes me the most excellent meals, and she keeps my wife happy with mint tea and blue pills. I am not involved in trade! I am only ensuring my domestic tranquility. That is one of the more notable goals of Grantville. One which I have come to value and embrace."

"How much are you going to ask for the stick matches?" Adolph meant he was interested in buying a jar.

"I have no idea," Georg Seeberger said. "I'm not involved in commerce. Your house servant will have to go to the market and ask at the booth Hannah, my cook's niece, is running."

For several months, Professor Doktor Georg Seeberger continued to get sly snickers in passing and finally decided that the profit from the booth was not worth the embarrassment. When he told the cook that Hannah needed to find another job, Hannah countered with an offer to buy the booth and business. The down payment wiped out what she had saved for a dowry. She also needed a loan from her aunt. Seeberger was happy to sell. Hannah started sleeping in the booth. Shortly after this, the peddler enlarged his line to include kerosene and kerosene lamps. Hannah's booth became known in town as the kerosene booth, and Hannah's fortune was secured.

Delivering kerosene to various outlet points shortly became Hermann's main business. It continued to increase as the popularity of kerosene lamps grew, but he continued to carry the McAdams line of products.

In time Hermann proposed marriage, and Hannah accepted.

Cassini Runs Home

Robert E. Waters

"Nothing's ever been as fun as baseball." – Mickey Mantle

Perinaldo, Italy

1636

Giulia Crovesi held the letter from Grantville, written by her brother Antonio, in her hand. She wanted to tear it up and use it as a cloth to dry her teary eyes, but she refrained. For now, anyway.

"Read it again." Jacopo Cassini found a chair and sat down in their dining room. "Once more, if you please."

She unfolded the parchment and read it again, or rather, paraphrased it. "They are staying in Grantville," she said. "They are not coming back. Our son has apparently taken an interest in...baseball."

Jacopo furrowed his brow. "What is baseball?"

Giulia shook her head. "I do not know, my love. Antonio does not say what it is."

Jacopo sighed and rubbed his thick beard. "My word! Your brother is a presumptuous man-child, thinking he has the right to keep our son away from us."

"Now, now." Giulia dropped the letter on the dining room table and blinked away a tear. "Antonio has always been good to Giovanni. He has taken care of the boy more so than—dare I say—us." She paused to let her words sink into her husband's clearly agitated mind. She wagged a finger. "And don't forget: we allowed Antonio to take Giovanni to Grantville."

"Yes, but just to study his future and what he is destined to become. Not to stay indefinitely."

That was true. They had given strict instructions to Antonio: go to Grantville, study Giovanni's future, and then return promptly so that the boy could begin his training in astronomy, astrology, engineering, and mathematics. There was never any discussion about them staying in the so-called "up-time" town, the town and people who had, surprisingly, changed the course of history, not only in Germany, but in the world entire. At least, that's what the rumors indicated. The title on the top of the letter said "Koudsi Law Firm," so her brother must have found employment there and was now intent on staying.

We should have known, Giulia thought as she sat down next to her husband. *We should have known that such a devil place would infect our boy...and my brother.*

Yet, despite her anger and sadness at her brother's letter, Giulia couldn't help but feel a measure of guilt. It had always been Antonio who had taken up the role of father for Giovanni. Both she and Jacopo had been—how should she put it?—absent in the day-to-day direction and guidance of their son's development. They had, in fact, been terrible parents.

Jacopo sighed and leaned back in his chair, his rather ample stomach straining the buttons on his dark vest. "So, what do we do about this?"

Giulia was surprised that her husband would ask such a question. Normally, he was the one who made all the decisions in the household, but he was as confused about the missive as she was.

"Well,"—she picked the letter back up and rolled her eyes across the words again—"we have only one choice, my love. We must go to Grantville and bring our son home."

Game Three Against the Saalfeld Dukes
July 25, 1636

Giovanni was happy. They had beaten the Saalfeld Dukes two to one. *Joy of joys!* The Mountaineers had now won five games. One more game against the Dukes, and then they'd finish off the season against the Schwarzburg 4-Baggers, a team that they had lost to twice earlier in the season. The 4-Baggers were tough, *really* tough, and these last two games against them were in Schwarzburg. The thought of playing them on their own field sent a chill up Giovanni's spine. But, despite his concern, he was confident that the Mountaineers could pull it off. His team had proven themselves an excellent ball club. *We'll beat those 4-Baggers*, he thought, a smile on his face. *I'm sure of it.*

Uncle Antonio was waiting for him in the parking lot. He had promised to attend the game with Luca Shumpert, but he had not. Why? Neither he, nor Luca, nor Lucas for that matter, had attended. Giovanni had spent the entire game playing on third, and he had continually looked into the stands to see if his uncle had finally arrived. He hadn't.

Why not?

Giovanni waved at his uncle, "*Ciao*, Uncle. Did you see the game?"

Uncle Antoino stood there, staring blankly at Giovanni as he approached.

"Uncle?"

Uncle Antoino blinked and shook his head. "No, I'm—I'm sorry, Gio. I, ah, had other business to attend to."

Giovanni looked around the parking lot. "Where are Luca and Lucas? They didn't come either?"

Uncle Antonio paused, sighed, then said, "They had an important matter to address." He rolled his eyes, forced a smile. "Come, let us return to the hotel and get something to eat...and to drink."

As they walked, Giovanni couldn't help but talk. "What a game it was, Uncle! You should have seen it. Bottom of the seventh, we had two on base: Elias and Jerry. First and second. Then, Big Boy Powers comes up and hits a line drive right into center field. The Duke outfielder messes up the catch, and the ball rolls to the wall. Elias scores, and Jerry gets to third. I couldn't believe it, but Bobby actually got to second. As big and slow as he is, I wouldn't have imagined that—"

"Do you mind, Gio?" Uncle Antonio rubbed his forehead. "I have a terrible headache. No talking, okay? Let's just enjoy the pleasant weather and—"

"But, I have to tell you how we won. So, Jerry is on third, and James comes up. Two strikes right away, and then bam! He knocks one into left field. The Duke outfielder runs to get it, but he can't make it. The crowd goes wild. Jerry runs to home plate, and we win! Isn't that awesome?"

"Yes...awesome. Now, can't we just—"

"But I have more to tell you." Giovanni couldn't contain himself. "After the game, Coach Flannery said that, with our five wins, we have a real chance of making the championship game, and that—"

"Enough, Gio! I cannot listen to any more of your talk. Be quiet!"

Giovanni looked up at his uncle. He seemed flushed, angry, sad. He looked into his uncle's eyes. Were those tears? No, not tears exactly, but his eyes were certainly wet.

"What's wrong, Uncle?"

"Nothing!" Uncle Antonio said in a very curt manner. "Nothing at all. Let's just get to the hotel."

But Giovanni could tell that his uncle was lying. *Something's wrong*, he thought looking at his uncle's weary eyes. *Something's really*, really *wrong*.

The Higgins Hotel
July 26, 1636

Too little food and too much wine had given Antonio a hangover. Not that he couldn't handle it; he had had hangovers before. But Giovanni's incessant mumbling of an up-time song forced him awake.

"Good morning, Uncle," Giovanni said as he thumbed through his stack of library books. "You slept in late today."

Antonio grunted, cleared his throat, leaned over the edge of the bed, and spat into their chamber pot. A pot like this wasn't needed in the Higgins Hotel. Each room had a bath and toilet. But Antonio made sure the pot was near his bed in case he awoke nauseated and ready to vomit. Luckily, he only spat.

"What are you doing?" Antonio asked.

Giovanni flipped a page, held up the book. Antonio squinted, noticed a baseball player on the front, an old up-timer that Antonio didn't recognize. "I'm looking through this book, looking for information about home runs."

"Home runs?" Antonio cleared his throat again, but this time, he didn't spit. "What for?"

"After today's final game against the Dukes, we're heading to Schwarzburg to play against the 4-Baggers. And I think it's high time that I learn how to hit a home run."

An admirable desire, Antonio thought, but perhaps a bit misguided. Dare he think it, but his nephew was probably a bit too small and lacked the necessary strength to hit a ball out of the park. The boy should be focusing on singles, doubles, stealing bases, and all the things that a young man of his stature should pursue. Home runs were not practical.

But Antonio said nothing about his opinion on the matter. Instead, he got up, stretched, and put on the fresh clothing sitting on the chair next to the bed. "What time is it?" he asked as he pulled on his breeches.

"It's breakfast time."

A minute afterwards, there was a knock at the door. Giovanni answered.

Antonio buttoned his vest as a hotel staff member, carrying a large tray of food, came in and set the tray on the bed. "You ordered breakfast?"

Giovanni nodded. "Yes. Since you were sleeping so late, I thought I'd take care of it."

Antonio smiled. "Thank you, Gio. That was nice of you."

Giovanni handed the man a little money for a tip. The man nodded, said, "Thank you," and left.

Antonio helped Giovanni move the tray to the table. They sat down and began to eat.

A dozen concerns flooded Antonio's gray, sorrowful mind. Now that Luca's husband, Gerhart, had returned, what now? What should he do? What *could* he do? His affair with Luca was clearly over. With her husband back in town, their "relationship" was through. The thought of it made his head hurt even more.

"You're coming to the game today, right?" Giovanni asked.

"Yes, yes," Antonio said, annoyed and preoccupied. "I'll be at the game."

"Great. And I hope Lucas will show up as well. Coach Flannery was worried about him."

Antonio cleared his throat and took a bite of scrambled eggs. He huffed. "Well, no need to be concerned about Lucas. I'm sure he'll be at the game...in *fine* fashion."

Giovanni continued to prattle on about the upcoming game, but Antonio concentrated on his food, nibbling on a piece of buttered toast while the boy asked a question. "Uncle Antonio, are you all right? Uncle?"

Antonio shook his head, blinked, and said, "Yes, yes. Sorry. What were you asking?"

"I wanted to know when we will be moving in with the Shumperts. Are we going to do it before the end of the season or afterwards?"

Moving in with the Shumperts... Antonio felt a tinge of anger and embarrassment in his heart. *She lied to me....*

He shook his head. "We're not moving in with them."

Giovanni leaned back in his chair, his mouth open, a look of confusion on his face. "What...why not?"

"Because...just, because." Antonio wiped his mouth and stood, straightening his vest. "I've decided. When the season is over, we're going back to Italy."

Giovanni looked like he'd been punched in the gut. He looked as if he were about to cry. "Why? I thought we were staying in Grantville."

"Yes, well,"—Antonio straightened his clothes—"we're not staying here. Living with the Shumperts is no longer a good idea."

"Why?" Giovanni shouted the question, but Antonio did not answer it. "You promised that we would stay here."

"I never promised."

"You did! And now you are going back on your word!"

Antonio looked around the room for his briefcase. "Where's my briefcase? I thought it was on the table. Where is my—"

"Answer me!"

Antonio turned to Giovanni, a look of real anger on his face. "Watch your mouth, boy. You do not demand anything. I'm your father...I, well, I'm not your father. I'm your uncle, your guardian, and I've decided. We will go back to Italy as soon as the season is over. Now, I don't want to hear another thing about it."

Giovanni was sobbing. He wiped his eyes. "But...why? Why are we leaving? I thought you liked it here."

"I do. But things have changed."

"What has changed?"

Antonio paused, looked at Giovanni. "Everything."

He walked to the bathroom and closed the door. He turned on the light, leaned over the sink, and looked at himself in the mirror. *Pathetic...utterly pathetic. Why didn't I tell him the truth? Why?*

Antonio turned on the water, filled his hands, and splashed his face. He turned his head to the closed door. Giovanni was still sobbing.

Please, God, do not let Gio run away again...

Game Four Against the Saalfeld Dukes
July 26, 1636

Giovanni's first inclination was to run, to hide again like he had done shortly after they had arrived in Grantville many weeks ago. But no, that was not who he was anymore. He was no longer an insecure, weak little boy. He was a Mountaineer, no matter what Uncle Antonio said or demanded. They were heading back to Italy when the season was over. Giovanni still felt like crying when he thought of that. But he would not run, nor would he hide away and bring tremendous grief and worry to his uncle. He was terribly upset, yes, but he had to show some level of courage, some level of maturity. His friends, and the *team*, were counting on him.

"Well, looky there." Jerry pointed. "Lucas is back."

And so he was, dressed in his uniform, smiling and ready to go.

"Where were you, young man?" Bobby asked, putting his hands on his waist as if he were a mother scolding her child. "We had to put Mr. Cassini on third yesterday. Luckily, we won. Where were you?"

Lucas walked into the dugout and took a seat on the bench. He removed his cap and wiped away the sweat on his brow. "I couldn't come yesterday. My father came back from the war."

The news hit Giovanni like a brick. *That's why we cannot live with the Shumperts.* Suddenly, his sorrow about leaving Grantville changed. He was no longer sad. He was angry.

But he said nothing. Big Boy Powers threw uncomfortable glances his way. Bobby knew that Uncle Antonio and Lucas's mother had been seeing each other; he had teased Giovanni about it not long ago. Now, their relationship was clear. *That's why we're going back to Italy. That's why.*

"Play ball!" The umpire shouted, starting the game.

The Dukes were up first. The Mountaineers got their gear and headed out to the field. All but Giovanni, who was pinch running today, if necessary. Now that Lucas was back, the third base position was filled.

As Lucas put on his cap to head out to third base, Giovanni could tell that Lucas wanted to say something to him. The boy kept looking at him, but Giovanni looked the other way, anger and confusion in his mind. Lucas sighed, grabbed his glove, and headed out.

Lucas's father is back, Giovanni thought as he watched Lucas head to third base. *He's back, and my uncle is hurt.*

* * *

Game four against the Saalfeld Dukes was in the second inning, but Antonio was reluctant to enter and find a seat. Luca and Gerhart were there. He knew they were because he had watched them go inside with their son Lucas, all happy and with arms around each other. Lucas had helped his father walk into the stadium. *What a delightful, loving, and helpful son!* He thought sarcastically. Antonio shook his head, rolled his eyes, and considered turning around and going back to the hotel. But he had promised Giovanni he'd be here, and despite his apprehension, he had to attend. This was the last home game of the season. The last two games were in Schwarzburg, and during those, he'd have to prepare for his and Giovanni's return to Italy.

The thought of going back to Italy was, to be honest, annoying. He had prepared himself—his heart, his spirit—to stay in Grantville. He had even written his sister Giulia that he and their son would be staying. Now, they weren't. Luca's husband was back, and as far as she was concerned, Antonio didn't matter anymore. *You could have, at least, given me warning that he had returned. That way, I wouldn't have been so crushed, so embarrassed, at your door.*

He bought a ticket and entered the stands. He paused for a moment to look over the stands and found a seat. Out of the corner of his eye, he saw them, Luca and her husband, sitting far to the right, side by side, Gerhart seemingly asking questions about a game he did not understand. They seemed so happy, so content sitting there, laughing and having a good time, and for a moment, Antonio took a step backwards and considered turning around and leaving.

But no, he would not do that. He would find a seat, far away from where they were sitting, and enjoy the game. Try to, anyway.

* * *

It was the bottom of the third inning, Mountaineers up, one out, Alex on first, Giovanni on second (pinch running for Bobby). Giovanni took a glance into the stands and saw his uncle. He was glad of that. Luca's mother and father were here as well but sitting further away so as not to distract Uncle Antonio in any way. Giovanni hoped his uncle wasn't distracted; he certainly was not feeling well about Lucas's father coming back. Giovanni didn't feel well about it either, but right now, he had to focus on the game. The score was tied zero to zero. Time to put some runs on the board.

Second baseman Elias Becker was at the plate. Elias was a decent batter, but he lacked the power of Bobby and the speed of Jerry. Bobby and Jerry were, indeed, the stars of the team, and Giovanni wished that he could be a star as well. Being a pinch runner was fine, but batting... that was the best. And the one thing that Giovanni hadn't done since he'd been a member of the Mountaineers was hit a home run.

He'd researched the subject but found little in the way of practical advice. The best advice was a quote from Rogers Hornsby who had apparently been a baseball player and a manager up-time. He'd played for several teams: the Cardinals, the Giants, the Braves, and many others. He had even coached those teams as well. His best advice for hitting home runs was simple: "Create bat speed." The faster you swing, the harder you will hit the ball. Good advice, indeed. But how could Giovanni create more bat speed? He wasn't Big Boy Powers, for heaven's sake. How could he do that?

But I will, he thought, as Elias swung his bat past the pitch and took a strike. *I will.*

One ball, one strike. Elias stepped back from the plate, adjusted his hat, his shirt, then stepped back up. The Dukes' pitcher leaned back, wound up to throw, and...*wild pitch*, off the catcher's glove. It bounced behind the catcher. He ripped off his helmet and went after the ball.

Giovanni ran to third base, easily reaching it before the Dukes' catcher found the ball. He considered trying for home plate but stopped a couple steps past third. He returned to the bag, and the Grantville crowd was delighted. So too Uncle Antonio, who was on his feet and clapping vociferously. Giovanni shot a glance towards Lucas's mother and father. They too were clapping.

He stepped off third and leaned towards home. Elias swung the bat a few times and prepared himself for the next pitch. The Grantville crowd continued to clap and cheer. Elias raised his bat and readied himself. The Dukes' pitcher threw the ball.

Elias struck the ball hard and high, knocking it into center field. Giovanni wanted to try for home again but knew the rules of the game: if the outfielder caught the ball, he would have to tag up before advancing. He waited, waited, waited until the ball flew across the sun. The Dukes' center fielder tracked back, back, held up his glove, and caught it.

Giovanni bolted towards home plate. He didn't even bother to concern himself with seeing if the center fielder was throwing the ball to get him out. He did not care. What mattered was reaching home plate. He ran, his eyes focused on the catcher who had his glove forward and up to catch Elias' sacrifice fly.

Giovanni dropped to the ground and slid, hands first, towards the plate. The catcher caught the throw and turned to tag him out as Giovanni's hand slid across home plate.

"Safe!"

The Grantville crowd cheered again as Giovanni stood, brushed the dirt off his shirt, and gladhanded his teammates waiting for him in the dugout. Lucas patted him on the back.

"Good going, Gio," Lucas said, but Giovanni kind of brushed off his hand and said nothing.

The Mountaineers were now up by one, Alex was on second, and Giovanni was very happy.

"Good job, Gio," Coach Flannery said. "You did well."

"*Grazie*," Giovanni said, then looked up at his coach. "Can I pinch hit in the next game?"

Coach Flannery considered it. He nodded. "We'll see."

* * *

Top of the seventh, and the Mountaineers were up two to one. One out, with a Saalfeld Dukes batter on second. Giovanni could see that Coach Flannery was worried. With a Duke on second, in so-called scoring position, a line drive into center field could bring the boy home and tie the game. The Mountaineers were not known for great defense, but they had to hold firm. With a loss in extra innings, the Mountaineers would be finished.

A Saalfeld Dukes batter stepped to the plate, adjusted himself for the pitch, and waited. The Mountaineers' best pitcher, Aaron Rollison Wendell, wound up the throw and sent it across home plate.

"Strike!"

Giovanni stood in the dugout and leaned against the fence. "*Andiamo,* Aaron," he said in Italian. "*Colpirlo.*"

Another pitch... "Strike!"

Two strikes. One more, and the boy on second would have a much harder time scoring and tying the game.

Aaron wound up the pitch and threw it. The Duke at the plate swung and hit the ball, but it was a low bouncer between second and third. Jerry leaped to his left, snagged the ball, collected himself, and threw the boy out at first.

Now, two outs, with one Duke still on second. Giovanni smiled. One more out, and the game would be over. But Armin Fischer was up, and Giovanni's heart began to beat.

Armin was truly the Dukes' best player. Kind of like Big Boy Powers, only a little smaller and not quite as strong on the swing. He was infamous for his singles and doubles, and he carried himself with a swagger reminiscent of the 4-Baggers' Baumann twins. Armin was formidable.

Aaron seemed worried as well. He'd pitched to Armin a couple times already, but now was the moment. Giovanni shouted out encouragement to their pitcher and banged the dugout fence as Aaron wound up the first pitch and let it fly.

Armin swung and sent the ball bouncing into center field.

The Dukes' player on second ran to third. Mountaineer center fielder Jimmy Shaver bobbled the ball, but recovered quickly and threw it to second baseman Elias Becker, who then threw it to third. But the Dukes' player on second had already rounded third and was racing home.

A foolish move, Giovanni thought as he shouted support from the dugout. *He'll never make it.*

For a moment, Lucas was confused as to where to throw the ball next, but the third base coach told him to throw it home, and so he did. Alex Dorrman caught it. The Duke runner paused, slid down, and tried to turn and run back to third. Alex threw the ball back to third. Lucas caught it and ran towards the runner to tag him out. The boy turned again and ran to home plate. Lucas threw the ball back to Alex.

Back and forth, back and forth, until the Dukes' player had no room to maneuver. He tried dodging, but Alex held out his arm and tagged the boy out.

The Grantville crowd went wild. Giovanni's throat hurt as he shouted his joy.

The game was over, and the Mountaineers now had six wins and four losses.

The Koudsi Law Firm
July 27, 1636

Antonio sat quietly at his desk, reviewing a few final briefs that Laura had handed him upon his arrival. His door was closed, but he saw shadowy shoes under the closed door. He knew who it was.

She knocked, then turned the knob and peeked in. She was trying to be pleasant. "Hello, Antonio. May I come in?"

He stared at her for a long moment, sighed, then waved her in. "Of course."

Luca entered, holding out two folders. "Laura wanted me to give you these as well. She forgot to hand them to you when you arrived."

Antonio accepted them and laid them on his desk. "Thank you, Luca." That was all he said.

She waited, but Antonio kept his eyes on the brief in front of him. Luca turned to leave, paused at the door. "I'm sorry, Antonio. I did not know my husband was coming back."

"Of course not." Antonio closed the folder, swiveled in his chair, and stared at her, an angry glint in his eye. "How could you have known? Although maybe you were a little too quick on the draw, as you Grantville people say. Maybe you should have waited a few more months to see if he would come back before deciding to crawl into my bed."

She closed the door, turned, and glared at him with eyes ready for tears. "What...you think I decided that he was dead too quickly? That I wanted him to be? That I am some kind of slut that just wanted to have a good time?"

She was speaking a little too loudly for Antonio's taste. Thankfully she had closed the door, but he was still worried that Laura would overhear and send them both away.

He held up his hands and tried to calm her down. "I'm sorry, Luca. I didn't mean to imply anything like that. It's just that, well, perhaps we got into this...*relationship* too quickly. Perhaps we should have waited a while." Antonio shook his head. "We should have waited."

Luca wiped away a tear. "I didn't know he was coming back. I swear."

"You could have told me he was back." Antonio stood and dared to step towards her. "You could have sent me a note or called the hotel and left a message." Antonio threw up his hands. "I got to your house and there he was. I didn't know what to say. I just stood there, like some blithering idiot."

"I'm sorry," she said again. "He came home the day before, late in the afternoon. He just showed up at our door. I couldn't believe it. I thought I was seeing a ghost, but Lucas was so happy to see his father." She lowered her chin. "We both were."

"Did you tell him about us?"

Luca raised her head and stared in shock. "Of course not. And I won't."

Antonio huffed. "And what about Lucas? He's a young boy. He knows about our...affair. He might, in time, tell his father."

It was clear that Luca hadn't thought of that. She stepped back against the door. She mumbled something in German, then said, "I pray to God that he doesn't."

"Of course." Antonio stepped away, returned to his desk, and sat down. "It doesn't matter anyway. Our time is over, and so be it. Giovanni and I will be returning to Italy in a few days."

"What?"

"That's right. We're going back to Italy." He sighed and returned to the brief. "There's nothing left for us here. I've already given Laura notice. Today is my last day."

"But Gio loves it here," Luca said. "You can't go back to—"

"It's decided!" Antonio said a little louder than he wanted, his anger and sorrow difficult to control. "And that's the end of it. Goodbye, Luca. I wish you and your husband and son good tidings."

Luca wanted to say something more, Antonio could tell. Instead, she sniffled, wiped away another tear, opened the door, and left.

Antonio waited until she had closed the door behind her. Then, he leaned back in his chair, cursed in Italian, and tossed a pen against the wall.

Game Three Against the Schwarzburg 4-Baggers
July 27, 1636

The Mountaineers left in the morning by train and made it to Schwarzburg in good time. Coach Flannery wanted to arrive early to get in some practice. It was needed. The 4-Baggers were the best team in the league; all they needed to do to make it to the championship game against the Jena Sliders was to win just one game. The Mountaineers needed to win both.

During their practice session, Giovanni dared to ask Big Boy for advice.

"What?" Bobby seemed confused. "You want to try to hit...a home run?"

"Yes," Giovanni said, preparing himself for batting practice.

"I have one question for you. Are you nuts?"

Giovanni groaned. "Come on, Bobby. I want to try to hit a home run today. Show me how it is done."

Bobby sighed and shook his head. "Okay, but I think this will be a waste of time. You ain't got the strength for it."

Giovanni ignored Bobby's insult and instead stared at him until the big boy gave in. Together, they took the field and began to practice.

Giovanni tried to take the advice that he had read in his books, but Bobby was, in fact, telling the truth: he had little upper body strength. And because of that, it would be difficult to swing the bat at the velocity defined in said books. But no matter. Giovanni was intent on proving that he could hit the ball as well as anyone else on the team. He had read the records of the top home run hitters in baseball: Hank Aaron, Babe Ruth, Willie Mays, among others. Giovanni could never hope to reach their career records. But that didn't matter. What he wanted was one, just one, home run, to show everyone that he could do it, that he, Giovanni Domenico Cassini, could win a game for the Mountaineers and put them into the championship. He *needed* to do this to stay longer in Grantville. If they lost both games, he'd be going home much sooner.

I don't want to go home.

Giovanni swung the bat as hard and as fast as he could, but still, no home run. One time, he hit the ball far into left field, but it was still several yards away from the fence. Eventually, Coach Flannery told him to stop trying to hit home runs. "If you keep swinging hard like that," the coach said, "you might pull a muscle in your arms. No more." Giovanni stopped, frustrated. He had to hit a home run... had to! Everything depended upon it.

In about an hour, the game would start. Giovanni saw that the 4-Baggers had arrived, and every single one of them looked larger and stronger than he, especially the two most formidable players on their team: Nikolaus and Johannes Baumann.

Giovanni shivered and worked his shoulders to loosen them up from all that power swinging. He was ready, despite a small soreness in his left shoulder. He wasn't about to let the coach know about it, however. If he did, the coach would likely keep him benched. Giovanni was scheduled again to be just a pinch runner. But not today. Today, he wanted to bat, and he'd figure out a way to make that happen.

The Koudsi Law Firm
July 27, 1636

Antonio was determined to read through all the briefs that Laura and Luca had given him. They contained information about Italian mercantile law, something that he was qualified to review and interpret. He'd finish the briefs today and then be done. Laura had already given him a fond farewell. Others in the law firm had done so as well. But not Luca. She remained at her desk and did not bother to speak to him again. Understandable, Antonio supposed, given the awkward encounter that they had had a few hours ago.

Another knock came to his door.

"Yes, what is it? Luca turned the knob and peeked in. Her face was clear and free from tears. "Sorry to bother you, Antonio, but there is a lady here to see you."

"Who?"

Luca shook her head. "She did not say."

Antonio sighed, closed the folder on his desk, and stood. "Very well."

What woman would be coming to see him during office hours? Antonio did not know. He knew so few people in Grantville, save for the hotel staff, family members of the Mountaineers, and Coach Flannery. Otherwise, he had kept to himself. *Maybe it's someone from the hotel*, he thought, standing and following Luca to the front of the office. *Maybe they're going to hand me a bill.*

But it wasn't. He knew who the woman was despite her elaborate dress and the hat that covered part of her face.

Antonio's heart leapt in his chest. "Giulia?"

The woman removed her hat and held out her hand for Antonio to take it. "Hello, my brother."

Game Three Against the Schwarzburg 4-Baggers
July 27, 1636

Giovanni tried ignoring Nikolaus Baumann's evil glare as he stepped off first base and leaned towards second. *He's trying to psych me out.* He chuckled to himself. *Funny term, psych,* he thought. To people in Grantville, it meant to scare someone, to make them uneasy. To down-timers, it could mean psychic abilities. Giovanni took another step towards second and remembered that his mother had once suggested that he pursue a career in astrology. He shook his head. That was not going to happen now. His time in Grantville had turned him away from such silly notions as divination and alchemy and other such "psychic" nonsense. At this point in his life, he would become either an astronomer, an engineer, a mathematician, or a famous baseball player. Giovanni hoped for the latter.

The 4-Baggers were leading one to zip at the top of the sixth inning. Giovanni was on first and Jerry on third with two outs. Left fielder Uwe Lange was up. Much like Giovanni, Uwe was a good runner, but not a great batter.

The 4-Baggers' pitcher wound up the toss and threw it straight across the plate. Strike one. Giovanni glanced towards Jerry on third. Jerry was standing fast, waiting for Uwe to (hopefully) pop a single into center field. Giovanni leaned again towards second base and waited.

The pitcher wound up again, and Giovanni bolted towards second. He focused his full attention on second base as the 4-Baggers' catcher threw the ball towards second to get him out. Giovanni stuck his right foot forward and slid. The ball reached the second baseman's glove. He tried tagging him out, but the swipe was too late. Giovanni's foot touched second right before being tagged by the glove.

"Safe!"

Now, two Mountaineers were in scoring position, and if Uwe could hit a single, they could go up two to one. Hopefully.

"Come on, Uwe!" Giovanni said, brushing himself off. "You can do this."

Uwe made his adjustments and stepped up to the plate, took a couple practice swings, bent at the knees, and settled in for the pitch. The 4-Baggers' pitcher reared back and released the ball, and Uwe hit it hard. The Mountaineers' fans in attendance began to cheer. Jerry ran to home plate, and Giovanni raced to third.

Uwe's hit was high and fast, and the center fielder on the 4-Baggers ran backwards to try to catch it. The sun was high and hot. Jerry touched home plate as Giovanni rounded third. The 4-Bagger went back, back, trying to shield his eyes from the glare with his glove. Back, back, back. The 4-Bagger raised his glove, stepped back, back...and caught the ball.

The Mountaineer fans deflated, and Giovanni crossed the plate. But, it didn't matter. With two outs, the outfielder's catch of Uwe's hit ended the top of the sixth.

Giovanni entered the dugout and sat down. Coach Flannery tapped his shoulder. "Good running, Gio. In the top of the seventh, you'll bat for Mr. De Jong."

Giovanni nodded. *Good*, he thought. *Now I can try to hit a home run.*

The Koudsi Law Firm
July 27, 1636

Antonio grabbed his sister's arm firmly and escorted her out of the building. "What are you doing here?"

Giulia pulled her arm away. "Let go of me. You do not grab me that way."

Antonio tried calming down. He sighed and rolled his eyes. "I'm sorry, but I'll ask again: what are you *doing* here?"

Giulia straightened herself and said, "We're here to get our son."

Antonio raised his brows. "Jacopo came with you?"

"Of course he did. Giovanni is our son, and we are taking him back home."

"Didn't you get the message I sent you?"

Giulia reached beneath the laces of her bodice and pulled out a slip of paper. "Yes. That is why we are here. We agreed that you would visit Grantville and nothing else. You were instructed to come back to Italy after your visit." Giulia put her hands on her hips and glared at Antonio. "Why are you staying here?"

Why? A good question if asked a few weeks ago, but the idea of staying in Grantville now seemed illogical and foolish. Antonio turned away from Giulia, a riot of mixed emotions swirling in his mind. "You needn't worry about us staying. Today is my last day at the Koudsi Law Firm. Once Giovanni's baseball season is over, we will be returning to Perinaldo as required."

"What is 'baseball'?" Giulia asked, walking to her brother and laying her hand on his shoulder.

Antonio chuckled. "You don't know what baseball is?"

"No."

He turned and stared into her eyes. His sister was a lovely woman, and one who, despite Jacopo being the so-called "man of the house," as up-timers might say, had a strong will. Antonio had no doubt that it was Giulia who had decided to come to Grantville and retrieve her son.

"Then tomorrow, sweet sister," Antonio said, a gleam in his eye, "we will travel to Schwarzburg by train, and you will see your first baseball game."

Giulia nodded, but Antonio could see confusion and apprehension in her eyes. "Train...what is that?"

Game Three Against the Schwarzburg 4-Baggers
July 27, 1636

It was the top of the seventh inning, and the 4-Baggers were still ahead by one. One out with Lucas Shumpert on first. Giovanni was next in the line-up.

"Focus your attention, Gio," Coach Flannery said. "All you have to do is get a single. Don't overexert yourself. Focus on the ball and swing the bat."

Giovanni was quite familiar with the fundamentals of baseball. "No problem, Coach." He stepped up to the plate. *But, I won't be hitting a single. I'll be hitting a home run.*

He held up his bat and waited for the pitch. The 4-Baggers' pitcher released the ball, and Giovanni swung the bat.

"Strike!"

He ignored Coach Flannery's calls to slow down his swing. Jerry Yost barked encouragement from the dugout, while Lucas eyed him from first base. Giovanni ignored Lucas's stare, raised his bat, and waited for the next pitch.

"Strike!"

Anxiety arose in the dugout as Giovanni tried ignoring Coach Flannery's calls to, again, slow down his swing. *I'm going to hit a home run, Coach. Just wait and see.*

Giovanni leaned over the plate, raised his bat, and waited as the 4-Baggers' pitcher readied for the throw.

He threw the pitch, a low fastball that Giovanni was not expecting. He'd watched this pitcher throughout the game, and consistently, the boy had thrown high fastballs. Not this time. This time, Giovanni watched as the ball barreled towards him at knee level. *Don't swing, don't swing,* was his first reaction. A ball so low, it'd certainly be called a 'ball' by the umpire. But his adrenaline was up, and he was determined to swing and go yard.

Giovanni swung at the pitch...and missed.

"Strike!"

In frustration, he walked to the dugout and tossed his bat to the ground. Jerry patted him on the shoulder, but Coach Flannery was less supportive. "You shouldn't have swung at that pitch, Gio. That was a ball for sure."

"What does it matter?" Giovanni barked.

"It'll matter for next year's tryouts," the coach said.

Giovanni plopped down on the bench and shook his head. "There won't be a next year for me. My uncle and I are going back to Italy after the season's over."

The dugout grew silent. Then, Jerry said, "You're going back?"

Giovanni nodded.

"Why?" Elias Becker asked.

"Because...just because."

A few more seconds of silence, and then Coach Flannery turned his attention back to the game. Next up for the Mountaineers was Bobby Powers.

Big Boy stepped up to the plate. Giovanni could see that the pitcher seemed nervous. The 4-Baggers' coach called for a brief timeout as he trundled out to the mound and discussed the situation with his pitcher.

"I wish you weren't going back," Jerry said.

Giovanni suppressed tears and said, "Me neither."

He expected Bobby to be walked to first base, but apparently the 4-Baggers' coach was allowing the pitcher to do his job. *Big mistake*, Giovanni thought. *Big, big mistake.*

And so it was. On the third pitch, Bobby swung the bat, as described by Rogers Hornsby, with the correct speed and power. The ball flew over the right fielder's head and out of the park.

Their fans went wild, and the Mountaineers were now up two to one.

Mountaineers Campsite
July 27, 1636

Giovanni had never seen his teammates so happy. Big Boy Powers' home run in the top of the seventh inning put them ahead, and there they stayed. The 4-Baggers managed to get a runner on second base in the bottom of the seventh, but their hitting afterwards was uncharacteristic of their skillful team. The Mountaineers won. Now, all they had to do was win the final game and move on to the championship against the Jena Sliders. Giovanni could feel the tension among his friends, but the most powerful emotion was joy, and he liked it. It was good to feel this way before heading back to Italy.

Coach Flannery had given them strict orders not to run off into the night, to not do anything dangerous or stupid. "And do *not* tip over any cows," he said with a glare in his eyes that made it clear that if anyone did something stupid like that again, he'd disband the team.

So, they sat around the campfire, talking "smack" as up-timers might say, and giving predictions about tomorrow's final game.

"I'll hit another home run," Bobby said, preening himself like a god. "And this time, it'll be hit farther than any I've hit before."

"Bullshit," Jerry said, punching a burning log with a stick and trying to keep his voice down so one of the chaperones wouldn't hear his foul words. "You might hit a homer, Bobby, but it ain't gonna be that far."

"You'll be lucky to hit one at all," Elias said, chuckling. "You'll probably strike out every time."

"Bite me," Bobby said, kicking a small chunk of charred wood at Elias. The boy evaded the chunk while everyone around the fire laughed. "I'll hit one, and I'll bet you five dollars on that."

"The odds of him hitting a home run aren't that bad," Giovanni said, looking up at the clear evening sky, blinking as the abundant stars blinked back. "He's probably going to be batting at least three times, maybe four. Recent 4-Baggers' pitching hasn't been that good, so I can see him going yard at least once."

Bobby pushed Alex out of the way, sidled up next to Giovanni, and patted him on the back. "See. This young man *knows* what he's talking about. He's weird, but he knows what he's talking about."

The boys were silent for a few seconds, then Jerry asked, "How do you know, Gio?"

Giovanni was surprised that his best friend didn't know, or remember, how Gio knew the odds. They knew who he was, or who he would become. *I'm Giovanni Domenico Cassini, the great astronomer. I discovered the Cassini Division inside Saturn's rings.* He hadn't yet, of course, but he would. That's what all the books in the Grantville library said. And he'd go on to do other things as well. It felt strange to him to know what he was going to do in the future. The feeling of knowing what he would and would not do in his long career seemed almost deflating. "Look, I discovered a huge gap in Saturn's rings," he'd declare as an adult. The people in the world would sigh and say, "Yeah, we already know that you found it," and then present an up-time book showing him a picture of the division. *Sometimes*, he thought, *I wish I hadn't come to Grantville. Discovering great things that I will do in the future seems anticlimactic now.*

But that was a foolish notion. He had come to Grantville, and here, he had discovered the greatest thing in all the world.

Giovanni shrugged. "I...I just know."

They continued talking and ribbing each other. Jerry and Elias got into a small wrestling match that had everyone in stitches. All but Giovanni, who quietly stepped away from the fire and found a fallen tree on which to sit. He could still hear the muffled voices of his teammates, but he was happy to be alone, just this once, to stare into the sky.

The Grantville books had given him vast knowledge of the Earth and the universe in which it resided, knowledge that many outside Grantville might consider blasphemous. Knowing that the Earth revolved around the sun and knowing that it was just one tiny planet in a vast galaxy and knowing that there were more galaxies in the universe than just the Milky Way did give Giovanni the information needed to excel as an astronomer in the future. Instead of simply discovering the Cassini Division which, in essence, was already well-known by many people, he could go on to do other, more important things in his life.

Giovanni slammed his foot into the soft ground below. *I don't want to be an astronomer or anything else. All I want to do is play baseball.*

"Hi."

Giovanni recognized the voice. He looked up at the boy standing next to him. "Hi, Lucas."

Lucas stood there for a moment. Giovanni slid right; Lucas sat down.

They both stared up into the smear of the Milky Way. Giovanni smiled. The stars were, indeed, brilliant and marvelous. The idea of being an astronomer, of studying and discovering new stars, and possibly new planets, did excite him. But, the idea was nowhere near as fun as baseball.

"I'm sorry my dad came back from the war," Lucas said. "I didn't know he was going to do that. Mama said he wasn't, but he did."

Suddenly, Giovanni felt guilty about shrugging off Lucas' hand during the last game against the Saalfeld Dukes. "It's okay. It's nice that you got your father back."

"Yeah." Lucas sniffled. "I'm glad he is back. But I'm sorry about you and your uncle not coming to live with us." He paused, then, "I wish you weren't going back to Italy."

Giovanni suppressed the urge to cry. He sniffled, then said, "Well, my uncle insists that we go back. He's quitting his job at the law firm, and we will be going back to Italy soon."

"Not if we win tomorrow's game and go to the championship."

Giovanni nodded. "Do you think we'll win?"

"If what you say about Bobby is true, we will."

In his mind, Giovanni imagined himself stepping up to the plate, winding up his bat, and waiting for the pitch. *Boom!* In his mind, he hit the ball so hard that it cracked in half. Both halves flew up into the sky, nearly touching the milky stream of stars above him. Both flew over the fence. Two home runs! The crowd went wild and the Mountaineers were heading to Jena. Huzzah!

Lucas smiled. "What are you laughing about?"

Giovanni rubbed his face, said, "Nothing, nothing." He stood. "What I said about Bobby is true. He will hit a home run tomorrow. And Lucas...so will I."

Game Four Against the Schwarzburg 4-Baggers
July 28, 1636

Antonio could tell from his sister's expression and her questions that she was intrigued by baseball. Perhaps not as enthusiastic about it as he or Giovanni was, but she was interested, nevertheless. The good news about arriving in Schwarzburg was that Luca and her husband were not at the game; apparently, Luca had a lot of work to do at the law firm. Antonio could now breathe freely and not have to brood about his ex-lover sitting mere feet from where he and his sister and her husband would reside. That was a comfort.

"Yes," Antonio said, answering her question, "seven innings, and each team plays in each inning, the so-called top of the inning and the bottom. Three outs, and then they switch. At the end of the seventh inning, whoever has the most points, wins."

"Hm," Giulia muttered. "How interesting. And you said that if the Mountaineers win this one, they go to the..."

"The championship game," Antonio said.

"And that means that you and Giovanni will stay here longer."

Antonio affirmed. "Yes, but only for a few days. The championship game will be in Jena."

"We will not be staying here for that long," Jacopo said. He seemed less interested in baseball than his wife. He also seemed annoyed by the number of people that were attending the game. "We must leave tomorrow so that Giovanni can begin his studies."

Antonio almost snapped at Jacopo. Instead, he smiled and said, "It would only be for a few more days, Jacopo. It's hardly something to worry about."

Jacopo grunted and tried to make his way through the crowd. Giulia looked at her brother with a smirk. Antonio returned the expression and then continued making his way through the crowd as well.

Antonio didn't want to be in Grantville any longer than Jacopo. It was time to go. Time to return to Italy and hopefully, if God was kind, start a new life. But a few extra days was nothing.

If they win this game, Jacopo, Antonio thought as he watched Giovanni's father find seats in the makeshift bleachers, *we're staying for the championship. I owe Gio that much.*

* * *

Giovanni couldn't believe what he was seeing. "Is that... Mama, Papa?" He blinked and shook his head to ensure that he wasn't imagining things. He looked again. Yes, it was. His parents were at the game. And Uncle Antonio as well.

His rush of joy was nearly explosive. He didn't bother telling the coach or anyone else that his parents were here. He simply ran to them, weaving his way up the bleachers, evading all the people trying to find seats. His mother put out her arms to catch him.

"Oh, Giovanni!" Giulia gave her son a strong squeeze. "How we have missed you!"

"Mama," Giovanni said, "why are you here? I—I didn't know you were coming."

"We're here to take you back home"—Jacopo patted his son on the head—"after you're done here."

"*If* they lose," Antonio interrupted. "But, if they win—"

"We're not just going to win, Uncle," Giovanni said. "We're going to crush them."

"Crush...them?" Giulia shot a glance at Antonio, concern in her eyes. "I don't understand."

He chuckled. "It's an up-time expression. It means that they are going to win by a large margin."

Both Giulia and Jacopo gave their son another hug and peck on the cheek. "Go now, Gio," Giulia said. "Play your game, so that we may watch."

He hugged his mother again, then turned and went back to the dugout. He was happy that all three of them were here. It was like a dream. The idea of going back to Italy left a bad taste in his mouth, but he was happy that his parents were here, watching the game. Watching him play baseball.

He was honored, and today, he would make them proud.

* * *

It was the bottom of the second inning, and the game was tied one to one. Bobby hadn't hit a home run, but he had driven the ball hard into center field for a single. Jerry had then stepped to the plate and hit another, sending Bobby to third. A sacrifice fly from Uwe had gotten Bobby home, but the Mountaineers made no further runs. The 4-Baggers had tied it up in the bottom of the first with a single by Nikolaus Baumann, and unfortunately, the Mountaineers had not scored a run at the top of the second.

So, bottom of the second, one out. Running from first to third had strained Bobby's ankle, and so Giovanni was subbing for him on first. In a difference from major league rules up-time, Bobby's sore ankle didn't mean that he couldn't bat anymore, but Coach Flannery didn't want their best hitter to play first and wear out his leg. Giovanni stood on first with one of the 4-Baggers who had hit a single.

Is he cursing me in German? Giovanni wondered as the boy mumbled phrases like "*Iss Scheiße*" and "*Schwaches Italienisch.*" He didn't understand what the boy was saying, but no matter. Giovanni gave it right back: "*Mordimi, cane tedesco.*"

Johannes Baumann stepped up to the plate, and Giovanni's heart sank. Brother Nikolaus was a good batter, but Johannes was the best of the 4-Baggers. His record of home runs eclipsed even Bobby's. The runner on first snickered at Giovanni and said something again in German.

"Bite me!" Giovanni said, taking a cue from Mr. Powers. "He'll strike out."

But Johannes did not strike out. On the third pitch, the young Baumann boy hit the ball hard and high. Center fielder James Shaver ran back, back, his eyes constantly tracking the ball as it flew towards the wall. Back, back, back. James put up his glove and tried to catch it, but his glove missed by inches. Home run!

The 4-Baggers were now up three to one, and Giovanni ached to be up at that plate, punching balls into center field.

* * *

"So," Giulia said, "that was a home run?"

Antonio nodded, with a slight ache in his gut. "Yes, and now the 4-Baggers are winning."

There was still plenty of time left in the game, and it was very possible that the Mountaineers could tie it up and win it. But the odds of that happening...Antonio couldn't think about it. He tried figuring out the odds, just like Gio might do, but he had more important matters to attend to.

"Duck!"

Antonio grabbed his sister and pushed her down into his lap. He shielded her head, neck, and shoulders as a foul ball ricocheted into the bleachers and struck the seats behind them. The people behind them ducked for cover as well but lost their drinks and hot dogs as the ball slammed into the bleachers and made a mess. Antonio's back was splashed with beer, but thankfully, the ball bounced up and over the seats.

"Are you all right?" He asked Giulia as he helped her recover.

She nodded. "I'm fine."

"And that, dear sister, is a foul ball." Antonio almost felt like laughing.

"My word!" Jacopo gripped his chest while collecting himself as well. "We could have been killed!"

"Unlikely," Antonio said. "Injured, yes, but killed? These young boys can't hit the ball hard enough for that."

"There should be a wall in place to stop these foul balls, as you call them, from flying into the seats." Jacopo leaned over and picked up a piece of hot dog. He thought about eating it, then handed it back to the man behind him.

"The Mountaineers' field has a fence that helps protect the fans from foul balls," Antonio said. "Right behind home plate." He grunted. "But I guess the 4-Baggers think that's too soft. I guess they prefer their fans to get struck by the ball."

"Monstrous!" Giulia straightened her dress and sat back down.

The next 4-Bagger batter skipped the ball right into Jerry Yost's glove. He threw it to second, and then, the second baseman threw it to first. Double play.

The second inning was over, and now, Antonio anxiously hoped that Giovanni would step up to the plate.

Give him at least another chance to bat, he thought, *before we go home.*

* * *

Coach Flannery had not established Giovanni as a DH or pinch hitter, but as a pinch runner. Probably for Bobby. He had done so many times in the past, so the idea of it was not offensive. But, this was the last game of the season...maybe. He needed to step up to the plate, wind up the bat, and take a shot. Before it was all over.

"Can I pinch hit for someone, Coach?" Giovanni asked in a kind of squeaky voice, fearing that, if he pushed too hard, Coach Flannery would snap at him.

The coach looked at him and nodded. "We've got a lot of game left, Mr. Cassini. We'll see."

Giovanni sat back down and watched the game. Lucas, Uwe, and James were up.

Lucas hit a bouncer to second base and was thrown out at first. Uwe reached first base on an error by the 4-Baggers' shortstop. While James was up at the plate, Uwe tried to steal second base, but was thrown out on a controversial call that sent Coach Flannery onto the field to argue with the ref. Things got heated, and Giovanni worried that Coach Flannery would be thrown out of the game. But Flannery, realizing that he might have taken things too far, backed off and returned to the dugout. Giovanni could hear his coach curse beneath his breath as he returned.

Jerry slid over to Giovanni. "Hey, do you think you can come to my house before you go back to Italy?"

Giovanni shrugged. "I don't know. Maybe. But, my mom and dad are here, and I don't think they want to stay for long."

They sat together in silence, watching James at the plate.

"Well, I hope you can. I'd like to have you over once more."

Giovanni nodded and placed his hand on Jerry's shoulder. "Me too."

On the fifth pitch, James swung hard and knocked the ball high into right field. He took off towards first, but the ball fell comfortably into the right fielder's glove. The 4-Baggers' fans cheered and clapped; the Mountaineers' fans stayed silent.

It was now the bottom of the third, and the Mountaineers were still down three to one.

* * *

Because Jacopo had held a ruined hot dog, his desire to acquire one fully intact grew strong. "Let's get hot dogs and something to drink," he said.

Antonio would have preferred to sit and watch the game, but he sighed and nodded. "Very well. The concession stand should have them."

He helped his sister down from the bleachers; her ample dress prevented her from moving quickly. Antonio could tell that she was sweating and made it a point to direct her under the roof of the concession stand so that she might find some comfort.

When Jacopo smelled the hot dogs, he ordered two. Antonio ordered one, as did Giulia. For drinks, one could order beer or water. Jacopo ordered a beer; Antonio and his sister ordered water with tiny bits of ice.

As they were walking back to the bleachers, Giulia paused to watch her son on first base, and in her eyes, Antonio noticed, he was marvelous. He dove to catch a ball shot between first and second and managed to reach first base before the 4-Bagger player touched the bag. The Mountaineers' fans cheered Giovanni on for his quick response.

Giulia chirped. "Oh, he's very good, isn't he?"

Antonio nodded. "He has improved considerably in the past few weeks."

They made their way into the bleachers. Giulia sat down with Antonio at her side. She took a bite of her hot dog and a cool sip of water. Then, she leaned over to her brother and whispered, "You know, maybe you and Gio should stay in Grantville."

Hearing those words, Antonio spilled his water and nearly choked on his hot dog.

* * *

It was now the top of the fifth with one out, and Elias Becker stepped up to the plate. The score was still three to one. Bobby Powers was up after Elias, and the pressure and anxiety in the Mountaineers' dugout were palpable.

"Hit a home run, Bobby," Giovanni said.

"You know I will." He winked and walked to the batter's box.

If Bobby hit at least a single, then Giovanni would pinch run for him. But of course, no one was hoping for just a single.

The Mountaineers' fans cheered Elias on as he swung and took a strike. The 4-Baggers' pitcher, Armin Bartel, was considered by many to be one of the finest in the league, though he had pitched now for a couple of innings and seemed to be growing tired. At least, that was what Giovanni observed. Armin was throwing low and inside. All Elias needed to do was just wait and get a walk to first. Then, let Bobby pop one out of the park. That was most possible.

But Elias was swinging the bat and ignoring Coach Flannery's calls to hold. Elias swung again, but this time, he clipped the ball off the pitcher's mound and took off towards first base. The shortstop moved forward, scooped up the ball, and tossed it to first.

"Out!" Shouted the first base umpire.

The Mountaineers' fans deflated, and Coach Flannery had a few stern words to say to Elias. Giovanni sat back down on the bench and ignored the coach's little temper tantrum. What he was saying to Elias didn't matter. What mattered now was the boy marching to the plate.

As Bobby prepared himself for the first pitch, Giovanni tried to recalculate in his mind the odds of Big Boy hitting a home run. One to one? Three to one? Four to one? He couldn't quite decide, the emotions in his mind and body distracting his thoughts. The chances were good, however, no matter the odds, and he jumped up again and cheered Bobby on, despite the big boy being, in Jerry's words, "a total dick."

First pitch, ball. Second was a ball as well, low and inside. Giovanni could see the muscles grinding away on Coach Flannery's face as he hoped and prayed that Bobby would simply ignore the pitches and get a walk. But even Giovanni knew that wasn't going to happen. Elias Becker might have made an error swinging the bat, but not Bobby. He was a different kind of batter.

The third pitch was a strike, and Giovanni's heart raced. "Come on, Bobby," he shouted, clapping his hands. "Go yard!"

Next pitch, a ball. Now, three balls, one strike. Bobby wound up his bat, leaned over home plate, and waited.

The pitch was another low slider, but Bobby swung and struck it hard, hard enough for it to fly up into center field...and over the fence.

Giovanni sat down on the bench and smiled as the Mountaineers' fans went bonkers.

I was right.

* * *

"I'm not saying that you have to stay in Grantville," Giulia whispered to try to keep her husband from hearing her and Antonio's conversation, "but it's clear to me that my son has found something that he truly likes doing. I don't know if this game, this baseball, will be enough to provide him a life and a career, but why take him away from it? Why not let him keep playing?"

Antonio appreciated the comment, but if he stayed in Grantville, his situation would likely take a turn for the worse. *I had an affair with a married woman*, he wanted to tell his sister, but refrained. *If I stay and her husband finds out, he might challenge me to a duel.* Antonio was no military man, no marksman. He'd be dead for sure, and the chance of Luca's husband finding out at some point was quite high. *Lots of gossip in Grantville.*

"Maybe you and Jacopo can stay with him," Antonio suggested, "and I can go back to Italy."

Giulia looked over at her husband who was preoccupied with finishing his second hot dog. She shook her head. "No. I'm afraid that cannot happen."

* * *

It was the bottom of the sixth, with two outs and one 4-Bagger on first, a young German lad named Christoph Weber who was one of the finest base stealers in the league. Giovanni was nervous. Pitcher Aaron Wendell was on the mound, and he had a tendency to toss the ball to first in order to keep the stealer in his place. The problem was Aaron sometimes made wild throws, high and over the first baseman. A taller fellow like Bobby could snag such a high throw, but not Gio.

Nikolaus Baumann was at the plate. Coach Flannery called a time out and went to the mound to discuss the situation with Aaron. Giovanni had a moment to reflect.

He looked into the bleachers where his uncle and parents were sitting. Mama had acquired a parasol to help shield her from the hot sun. His uncle and father were bent forward, talking across his mother's lap. What they were discussing, he did not know. Was Uncle Antonio trying to convince his parents to let him stay in Grantville? Were his parents going to stay in Grantville with him? That would be most ideal, and then, he'd be able to show them around the town, the school, and most importantly, the library, where the greatest knowledge of the universe was contained. And, of course, sports. Books about football and basketball, hockey and soccer, and the most important sport of all: baseball. Oh, how he'd revel in telling them stories about Mickey Mantle and Rogers Hornsby and Babe Ruth and Reggie Jackson. All the great up-time players he had studied and been inspired by. Would they be impressed? Giovanni shook his head. Hard to know.

Coach Flannery finished his talk with Aaron and returned to the dugout. Nikolaus Baumann stepped back up to the plate and readied for the pitch.

Based on Aaron's first throw, it was clear that Coach Flannery wanted to walk Nikolaus to first. The first two pitches were balls. Giovanni took a step back from first base, carefully watching Christoph take nearly three steps off first towards second. *Foolish move*, Giovanni thought. *They're walking Baumann*, dummkopf. *Stay on first.* But the arrogant boy, too confident in his ability to steal second base, stayed off the bag and waited.

Aaron looked to throw again to home plate, but suddenly, he turned his body and tossed the ball to first. Giovanni, his mind moving at breakneck speed, stepped forward, leaped at least a foot over the bag, and caught the ball. Christoph, having leaned too far towards second, tried to turn back to first. He reached his hand out and propelled himself forward. But Giovanni dropped down on first and tagged Christoph out.

The 4-Baggers' fans groaned. Giovanni winked at Christoph, stood straight and, like many up-time players, tapped his chest, then pointed to God.

* * *

"Mr. Cassini," Coach Flannery said. "You'll bat for Elias."

Giovanni wanted to jump for joy, but it was clear that Elias didn't like the fact that he was being benched for not listening to the coach's direction in the fifth inning. He avoided eye contact with Elias and moved to claim a bat. He wasn't the first player up. Jerry was up first at the top of the seventh.

Of all the players on the Mountaineers, he'd miss Jerry the most. They'd been friends since the beginning. He'd gone over to Jerry's house many times. How could they remain friends with so much distance between them? Giovanni didn't know, but surely there was a way. There had to be a way.

The score was still three to two. The top of the seventh was the crucial inning: if the Mountaineers didn't tie the score, or pull ahead, it was over. The pressure was mounting, and Giovanni could tell that their fans were anxious.

Jerry stepped to the plate. Jerry was fast and agile. His chances of reaching first base before being thrown out were high. All he had to do was knock the ball somewhere between the bases, tear off towards first, and gain a single. Giovanni had no doubt that that would happen.

"Come on, Jerry!" Giovanni shouted. "You can do this!"

Jerry turned to Giovanni, tipped his hat, and prepared for the pitch.

"Strike!" The 4-Baggers' pitcher threw a fastball right over the plate. Jerry prepared for the next pitch.

Giovanni clapped and provided verbal support for his friend. It worked. Jerry hit the ball between second and third. The 4-Baggers' shortstop tried to snag it but failed. The ball bounded into left field. The left fielder scooped it up and tossed it to second. Jerry reached first and tried going for second, but paused and scampered back to first before the ball was tossed to the first baseman. He was safe, and the Mountaineers' fans cheered.

Next up, Alex Dorrman. Alex was a good batter, but Giovanni could tell that he was apprehensive, nervous. Who wouldn't be? It was the top of the seventh, and the Mountaineers needed one run to tie the game. Two runs would put them ahead. Everything was riding on this inning, and Alex's face revealed the stakes.

"You can do this, Alex," Giovanni called from the dugout. "Come on!"

The decibel level in the bleachers increased. Alex stepped up to the plate, made a couple of practice swings, and then leaned over the plate, ready for the pitch. The 4-Baggers' pitcher gave a couple nods to his catcher, wound up his pitch, and let it fly.

Crack! Alex hit the ball between first and second base. The second baseman attempted to snag it like the shortstop had tried to do with Jerry's single, but the ball bounced over his glove and into center field.

Jerry slid into second base and considered trying for third, but the center fielder had been shallow and thus scooped up the ball quickly, preventing Jerry from reaching third. Alex, however, made first base right before the centerfielder threw the ball to first. He was pronounced safe.

The Mountaineers' fans were ecstatic now. No outs with players on first and second. The odds were in their favor to score at least one run, if not more. Giovanni did the math in his head as Johannes De Jong stepped from the batter's box to the plate.

"Okay, Gio," Coach Flannery said, "hit the box."

As Johannes stepped to the plate, Giovanni stepped into the on-deck circle. He wanted to watch the game but knew that he had to take a few practice swings before stepping to the plate himself.

Johannes was certainly not the best batter on the team, but he had good vision and could run reasonably well. Or, perhaps he'd get four balls and load the bases. That would be very, very nice.

"Ball!" the umpire shouted, and Johannes wound up his bat for the second pitch.

Another ball, and Giovanni swung his bat confidently in the box, expressing his satisfaction. *Two more balls, and the bases are loaded.*

The 4-Baggers' pitcher tried a slider, but Johannes swung and struck the ball in between second and third.

"Go, Johannes, go!" Giovanni shouted over the roar of the crowd.

But, unlike Jerry's single, the 4-Baggers' shortstop caught the ball, tossed it underhanded to second, and took Alex out. The second baseman then threw the ball to first. Johannes was fast, indeed, but not fast enough. Right before he touched the bag, the first baseman caught the ball, and the first base umpire shouted, "Out!"

The Mountaineers' fans deflated. Now, there were two outs with Jerry on third, and Giovanni was up.

As he walked to the plate, Giovanni glanced into the bleachers. His mother gave him a short wave. He waved back and tried to smile. His stomach tightened. He felt like throwing up.

He didn't throw up, though everything was on the line now. Two outs, and Jerry, his best friend, was on third. A single would send Jerry home and tie the game. But, a home run...*yes, a home run. That's what we need...and I'm going to deliver it.*

Giovanni stepped up to the plate and waited for the first pitch.

* * *

Giulia gripped Antonio's arms tightly. She buried her face in his sleeve. "I can't watch...I can't."

Her nails pierced his skin, and Antonio winced. He tried prying his sister's hands off his arm. "It is okay, Giulia. Come now. Everything will be all right. Watch your son at bat."

Finally, Giulia relented, calmed, and returned to her normal, proper sitting position. Antonio could see that Jacopo had finally finished his hot dogs and was almost as anxious as his wife. He was glad to see both his sister and her husband genuinely concerned about Gio's moment at the plate. In the past, their interest in their son had been rather less impressive. They loved their son, indeed, but the demands of their own lives had limited their ability to spend quality time with him. Hence the reason that Antonio had taken Gio to Grantville. But now they were engaged, on the edge of their seats, waiting and hoping for something good, something positive, to happen to their son.

Antonio took his sister's hand and gripped it tightly.

Gio took his first swing.

* * *

"Strike!"

The pressure seemed unrelenting to Giovanni. *Should I swing? Should I not? What would Antonio think if I didn't try? My Mother? Father?* The weight of the whole world seemed to press on his head, and he considered simply stepping away, not doing anything at all. But no. Jerry was on third, and if he could just hit the ball hard enough to bounce it into center field, left or right, then it would all be tied up.

Jerry clapped and shouted from third base. "Come on, Gio. You can do this!"

Jerry's confidence bolstered Giovanni's resolve. *Yes...I can do this.* He wound up and waited for the pitch.

He hesitated, and the ball flew outside the strike zone. "Ball!"

One ball, one strike. He stepped away from the plate, tapped his bat against his shoe, and stepped back up.

Jerry leaned off third. The Mountaineers' fans were loud and hopeful.

The ball was tossed, a fastball low and inside.

Giovanni swung and hit the ball harder than he had ever hit a ball.

For a moment, he hesitated. He stood there looking at the ball fly up, up into right field. He couldn't believe it. He'd hit it like Bobby hit balls, and for a few seconds, he just stood there and watched it.

"Go!" Coach Flannery shouted. "Go!"

Giovanni tossed his bat aside and ran towards first.

The ball was struck so high and so hard that the 4-Baggers' right fielder hesitated as well, never imagining that someone like Giovanni Cassini could hit a ball so hard. But he recovered quickly and fell back as the ball arched towards the fence.

This is it, Giovanni thought as he neared first. *This is my home run. We'll win, and I will be even more famous than Bobby.*

A thousand accolades swarmed through Giovanni's head as he imagined himself a star, the winner of the season and securing himself a longer stay in Grantville. Oh, how wonderful it was as the ball arched down towards the fence.

But the 4-Baggers' right fielder was fast. He fell back, back, towards the fence, angling his glove at the right moment. He jumped, his arm extended, his glove out and open.

Giovanni was ecstatic. *It's gonna miss his glove...it's gonna miss his glove...*

But it didn't. The outfielder rose up at just the right time and caught the ball as it tried to soar over the fence.

The 4-Baggers' bench poured onto the field, and their fans went wild. The game was over. The 4-Baggers' had won three to two.

* * *

"You did very well," Giulia said as she gave Giovanni a warm hug. "We are proud of you."

Proud of me? Why? How can you be proud of failure? Giovanni wanted to say out loud, but his emotions, the combination of anger and sorrow, overwhelmed him. After the game, he tried speaking with Jerry and Lucas and even Bobby, but they too were upset and disappointed at what had happened. Giovanni had foolishly tried to hit a home run, just like he had tried against the Saalfeld Dukes, and he had failed. He had let his whole team down, and now, it was over. The season was over.

"You did well, Gio," Antonio said as they climbed into a carriage that would take them to the train station and back to Grantville. "You've nothing to be sorry about."

They climbed into the carriage. Giovanni sat near the window, looking at the 4-Baggers' field while watching his friends find their parents and make their ways home as well. Some of them looked his way. He wanted to wave at them and smile, but he couldn't. It just didn't feel right after what he had done.

Time passed, then Giulia said, "Giovanni. Your uncle and I have talked, and...if you want to stay in Grantville, you may."

"What?" Jacopo said, quite surprised. "You did not discuss this with me, my dear."

Giulia turned to her husband. "Antonio has agreed to stay with Gio if he chooses to do so."

"But...we agreed that we were coming to Grantville to take our son home. I did not come all the way to Germany just to—"

Giulia put her hand on Jacopo's arm and spoke gently. "Please, Jacopo, listen to me. What better place to become an astronomer, or a mathematician, or even an engineer than in Grantville, a town from the future? Gio will have an opportunity to study all of the up-time knowledge that he would never receive in Italy. It is the right place for him to be."

Jacopo shook his head "No, my love, there is some information in Italy that has come from Grantville: books, papers, other things. Surely more knowledge will come to Italy over the next several years."

"Perhaps." Antonio joined the conversation. "But nowhere in all the world would Giovanni be able to study and learn as much as in Grantville." Antonio sniffled and wiped his nose. "If he wants to stay in Grantville, I'm willing to stay as well."

The carriage grew silent. His mother then said, "Well, Giovanni, do you want to stay in Grantville? It is your choice."

My choice? For a moment, Giovanni's mood shifted to delight. But then he looked at his father whose expression was not pleasant. He then looked at Uncle Antonio, and although he had apparently decided to stay in Grantville, Giovanni could tell that his desire to do so was...limited. He could tell by his uncle's eyes that he truly did not want to stay. *He's only doing this for me.*

Giovanni looked through the window at the 4-Baggers' field as it slowly disappeared from his sight.

He turned and looked at his uncle and parents. He shook his head. "No, Mama. My father is correct. There is no reason for us to stay in Grantville anymore." He held back a tear. "It's time to go home."

Higgins Hotel
July 29, 1636

Before leaving, they had breakfast at the hotel, and then Antonio paid his bill in full for their stay. Giulia offered to pay some of it, but Antonio refused. "The Koudsi Law Firm was generous in their payment to me," he said. "Thank you, but I can manage."

Giovanni packed his satchel. He packed his clothing and some of the baseball cards that he had acquired. He had left his bat and glove at the 4-Baggers' field. His uniform? He packed that too, though he wasn't sure that he should. *Perhaps I should give it back to Coach Flannery*, he thought. But it didn't matter. They were leaving, and the odds of the coach showing up upon their departure were, well, slim.

"Are you ready?" Uncle Antonio asked.

Giovanni hoisted his satchel onto his shoulder, nodded, and sighed. "I'm ready."

Walking down the stairs to the lobby felt like a sad processional, a *pavane*. Giovanni imagined hearing sad music as he walked, step by step. Uncle Antonio placed his arm on Giovanni's shoulder. "It'll be all right, Gio. We had a great time here in Grantville. I dare say that I'll never forget it."

Giovanni nodded. "Neither will I."

They reached the lobby. His mother and father were waiting. Mother smiled and gave him a hug and a small kiss on his head. "There's someone outside who wants to see you."

Giovanni perked up. "Is it Jerry?"

Giulia shook her head. "No, more than that."

Giovanni dropped his satchel and stepped outside. There stood the entire Mountaineers' team.

Aaron, Alex, Elias, and Lucas. Big Boy Bobby and James, Johannes, and Uwe. And Jerry. All of them, standing in front of their carriage.

"Attention!" Coach Flannery shouted, and the boys snapped to. "Present bats!"

One by one, each boy fell in line, half on one side of the walkway to their carriage, half on the other. Together, they raised their bats and held them over the walkway, all bats point-to-point, like an archway.

Coach Flannery stepped up to Giovanni. He was holding a ball and glove, a bat, and a wrapped package. "Mr. Cassini, for your time with us, I want to present to you these things to take back to Italy, so that you will never forget that you are, and always will be, a Mountaineer." Coach Flannery held them out for Giovanni. He took them, slowly, tears welling up in his eyes.

"Thank you, Coach," Giovanni said, a tear dripping down his cheek. "I...I don't know what to say."

"You don't have to say anything, young man." The coach put his hand on Giovanni's shoulder. "We just want to thank you for your contribution to our team."

"But...I didn't hit a home run in the game yesterday. I—"

"Don't worry about it. We finished the season with a winning record: seven and five. That's the first time in a long while that we've had a winning record. You did your best, and that's all that matters." Coach Flannery looked back at his players. "We're all proud of you, and we wish you the best. Now,"—he winked—"get going."

As Giovanni walked underneath the baseball bats, the Mountaineers began to chant, "Gio... Gio... Gio..." low and steady at first, and then louder as he reached the carriage. Once he was there, they lowered their bats and went to him, chanting his name and giving him strong, firm pats on the back. Bobby Powers hoisted him off the ground and gave him a big hug. "Don't tip over any cows in Italy, you tiny oaf."

Bobby let go, and Giovanni replied with a wink, "Bite me!"

Jerry stepped up and gave him a big hug. "Goodbye, Gio. Come back to Grantville sometime."

Giovanni nodded. "I will."

And then, Lucas stepped up. Giovanni wasn't sure how to say goodbye to him, but the boy smiled and Gio smiled back. "Sorry you guys couldn't stay with us, but, well, you know."

"Yes, I know," Giovanni said. "No problem, my friend. You just keep playing ball."

Even Antonio patted Lucas on the head. Then it was over. Giovanni climbed into the carriage, followed by his uncle, mother, and father. Their time in Grantville was over.

It was time to go.

* * *

Giovanni looked back at Grantville one last time. Then, the carriage rounded a corner and it was gone. Gone, perhaps forever. Jerry wanted him to come back at some point, and perhaps he would. Then again, maybe not. According to the books in the Grantville Library, Giovanni Domenico Cassini had moved to France. But not yet, not today. Today, he was heading home to Italy, and there he would stay for a long, long time.

Perhaps forever. He didn't have to abide by what the library books had said. He could make that decision on his own. His mother had said that he could stay in Grantville if he wanted to, and to some extent, he did. Staying in Grantville would have been wonderful. But, it was his choice, and he had decided to leave. And why?

Because he had an important thing to do in Italy.

Giovanni looked at his father. Jacopo was half asleep, his head going down, then up, and down again as the carriage wheels found potholes and rough patches on the road. His mother was awake with her hands locked together over her lap. She was looking out the window, watching trees and bushes rustle in the light breeze. Antonio sat next to the window as well, and Giovanni could tell that he was happy and unhappy at the same time. Glad to be leaving Grantville, and yet, sad about his unexpected breakup with Luca Shumpert. But it would be okay. There had to be a woman somewhere in Italy who would take a liking to his uncle. Antonio was a strong and confident man. He'd find another love, and when he did, Grantville would be nothing but a faint memory.

Giulia turned to Giovanni. "Well, my sweet boy, we're heading home. And soon, you'll begin your career as a great scientist." She smiled. "Are you excited?"

Giovanni looked at his mother and smiled also. "Someday, Mama, I may indeed become a scientist. But, not today, and not for a long, long time. I have more important things to do in Perinaldo."

"Oh, and what is that?"

Giovanni held up his glove, bat, and ball. He could not contain his joy. "I'm going to teach all of Italy how to play baseball."

A Guest At The New Year
Tim Sayeau

Bramall Hall, England
June 1635

Sir William Davenport stared at the oilskin packet held in the mercenary captain's hand. Behind that worthy was another mercenary holding the reins of his captain's horse.

When the troop appeared in the lane leading to Bramall Hall, Sir William had feared the worst. King Charles hadn't been the most phlegmatic of rulers before learning from the up-time town of Grantville of his beheading in early 1649. The arrest and execution of many future regicides (excluding Oliver Cromwell) hadn't calmed him nor his equally excitable wife Queen Henrietta.

Then came February 1634, when, at the instigation of Thomas Wentworth (Charles' then-chief counselor), a London mob attacked the king and queen as the royal couple sought to leave London for Oxford. Icy roads and panic resulted in a devastating carriage crash, killing her and permanently crippling him. Had Richard Boyle, Earl of Cork, not arrested Wentworth, the plot to murder the royal family and install Cromwell as lord protector might well have succeeded.

That the accusation against Wentworth was demonstrably false, that Charles and Henrietta were solely responsible for their tragic accident, and that Boyle was an amoral opportunist using the king for personal power and profit were clear truths only the imprudent voiced. Not when, thanks to French gold, the king and Boyle garrisoned thousands of mercenaries, gallowglasses, and worse throughout England.

These days, with Cromwell loose somewhere, perhaps in the north country, with Wentworth free in the Netherlands, with the up-time English Civil War increasingly likely to commence early, minor lords of the manor such as Sir William Davenport of Bramall Hall stayed heads down, thoughts hidden, choices—uncertain.

Now a troop of mercenaries headed directly to him, his family, his retainers.

Supposedly for benign reasons, but mercenaries, hah. *God in Heaven, I'll provide them with food and small beer, but I beg thee, Lord of All, have them willing to camp a mile or three away!*

That Captain Ebulus Crippen politely introduced himself and also dismounted from his horse meant this might end well, but count no man happy until he dies, call no mercenary friendly until he and his are gone.

As anxious faces peeped through ground and first-floor windows onto those assembled within the hall's main courtyard, Captain Crippen again held out his oilskin packet. "I assure you, Sir William, that though what is inside does indeed come from Grantville, no suspicion attaches to you and yours!"

Sir William Davenport blanched. "Captain Crippen, I assure you, all here are most loyal to King Charles—"

Crippen grinned, an old sword-cut on his face riding up, revealing yellow teeth, reddish-brown gums. "And I repeat, Sir William, we are not here for what you fear!" He shook his head. "Pardon the rhyme, sir. I meant no mockery!"

Moving a step closer in, he spoke again, as though imparting a confidence. "Sir William, what is inside is an envelope, a letter, directly from Grantville, from an up-timer! An utterly curious one, yes, but I assure you, 'tis only that, curious!"

Ignoring Sir William's near-faint, he stepped back. "Our commission here, Sir William, is solely to deliver you that letter! And to your good wife, whom I presume is the one watching us most anxiously from the entranceway there." Smiling, waving at the woman, Crippen again stepped back from Sir William.

With a surprisingly courtly bow, Crippen with both hands held the packet out toward Sir William. "Do accept it, Sir William, the day's already overlong, the road dusty, and having read it myself, I assure you, on my honour, sir, you will find it most intriguing, curious and intriguing!" He finished with another teeth-baring grin, the scar almost a second smile.

Concealing his thoughts that the only honour mercenaries usually had was silver and gold, Sir William opened the pouch. Inside was indeed the promised envelope and letter, a sign Captain Crippen's purpose here was as he claimed. Not proof enough to allay worry, but enough to warily proceed.

The envelope, creased and stained, featured on its right upper corner three large stamps, each marked with a red-ink circle, inscribed "Grantville WV 5-12-1635" in small letters. The stamps themselves depicted an attractive blonde, obviously an up-timer, wearing only a smile and a cloth of gold billowing sufficiently to promote attention whilst preserving modesty. She held in one outstretched arm and hand a pole, displaying the red-and-gold flag of the United States of Europe.

On the envelope front in sharp letters—Are those what up-timers call *typewritten*? Helpful, considering how some write—*It's called sand, you fools, use it when ink blots!*—was

Sir William Davenport

Bramall Hall

Bramall Hall Road

Duchy of Lancaster

Stockport England UK

"Uk?" He handed the oilskin pouch to Crippen, ignoring the writer wrongly placing him and his home in Lancaster, not Cheshire. *Three hundred sixty-some years, one should expect differences!*

"U. K.," explained the captain. "An abbreviation for 'United Kingdom.' Heed it not, 'tis immaterial."

Wondering who, what, England united with—*France? Surely Charles would not, would never...no, no questions!*—Sir William concentrated instead upon the envelope. There, in the upper left corner, was

Adina Daoud

306 Brush Run Street

Grantville, West Virginia County

USE 26573

Inside was one page, typewritten on both sides. As Captain Crippen and his command awaited, Sir William Davenport read what up-timer Adina Daoud thought important enough to write, er, type!

Adina Daoud

May 11, 1635

306 Brush Run Street

Grantville, WV County

USE 26573

To Sir William Davenport

Bramall Hall

Bramall Hall Road

Stockport, Duchy of Lancaster

England UK

Hello, Sir William! You don't know me, I don't know you, but I know of you, and that's why I'm writing to you. (Also, to those checking this letter because King Charles is paranoid: Hello to you, too, and please, if nothing else, at least tell Sir William what my letter is about.)

Sir William, I know writing to you will probably cause problems. I'm sorry, but I swear, I really have a good reason to!

Back in 1977, my parents and I toured Europe over summer vacation. We did the usual touristy things: saw Paris from the Eiffel Tower, watched the Changing of the Guard, kissed the Blarney Stone, saw Stonehenge, toured the Louvre, the Tower of London, etc., etc. (By the way, England really put on a show that year—it was Queen Elizabeth II's Silver Jubilee—celebrations all over!)

We also (my dad's really into ghosts and ghost stories and I am too!) went on a Haunted Tour of England. Up-time, England is called the world's ghostliest country, the Most Haunted Nation on Earth. Nobody's sure why, but the history, plus the cold and wet, maybe explains that. (Two words, Sir William, central heating!)

Part of the tour was at Bramall Hall, and I'm sorry, but here's where this gets bad. Really, really bad. You better sit down, that's how bad. Right, here goes.

Up-time, Bramall Hall had five ghosts. You maybe know some already, but there's two that shouldn't yet have happened. The Red Rider, the Ghost Room.

On a New Year's Eve, probably 1639 but nobody knows for sure, so I hope this is in time, a Red Rider—he's called that because he rode a horse, wearing a red-lined cloak—the rider, not the horse!—appeared out of a storm, asking for shelter. Everybody at Bramall Hall up-time says you were, are, a really good man, so you gave it.

In the morning, you were dead. Murdered. The Red Rider was gone, and since then, every New Year's Eve the Red Rider's ghost gallops on his horse up to Bramall Hall, disappearing just before the front entrance. That's bad, that's <u>nasty</u>, but I'm sorry, there's worse. I'm sorry, but there is!

Per the story, your wife, Dame Dorothy, didn't long survive your death. She died, and it's her ghost in the Ghost Room, the Paradise Room.

Sir William, I can't imagine what it's like to learn all this. You dead, your wife becoming a ghost, that's...a shock, it's a shock. I'm sorry for that, but here's why I'm writing.

Up-time, ghosts were, are, Big Business. Really, <u>Really</u> <u>Big Business</u>! There are ghost tours, ghost walks (people walk around at night where ghosts show up, and sometimes they do!), ghost watches (people stay in a place watching for ghosts; Bramall Hall holds one for The Red Rider every New Year's Eve), and that's fine. That really is.

Thing is, great as ghosts and ghost stories are, I think for those involved (Have you ever heard of happy people turning into ghosts? Cheery incidents creating ghosts? I sure haven't!) it isn't great, it isn't fine. It's horrible.

Now, probably, The Red Rider won't ever happen, Grantville's butterflied him away, but—maybe not. Plus, even if he never shows up, it's not like there's a shortage of guys like him, which is why I'm writing you, so you can watch out, take precautions.

As for the other ghosts, a child's sometimes heard crying in the chapel. There's a White Lady haunting the Plaster Room—she and her lover were murdered in Macclesfield Forest near the hall. Alice, the Maid of Bramall Hall, shows up in a russet gown in the entrance hall. She died there of shock on hearing her lover was murdered, also in Macclesfield Forest. (That place is dangerous!)

I don't know when those happened, nobody does. But, if you see a child crying in the chapel, please comfort him, her. Warn people, be careful in the forest. If there's a maid named Alice and she has a boyfriend, warn them too. Your wife, hug her, tell her you love her.

That's all I've got to say, Sir William. I hope it's good.

Sincerely,

Adina Daoud

Sir William Davenport looked at the letter. Turned it over, held it up to the sunlight, looking for what, he wasn't certain. Looked again at the letter, at one side, the other, checking inside its envelope. As emotions criss-crossed his face, he looked up, plaintively asking "Captain Crippen, what the, is this a, a—? What *is* this? *What?*"

Crippen grinned, the sword-cut again displaying his teeth. "Aye, quite surprising, isn't it?" Sobering, he added, "For you and your wife. That is her, is it not, still watching us there?"

This time, Sir William turned, regarding where Crippen pointed. "Yes, that is her, that is Dorothy." He waved reassurance to her; she again waved uncertainly back. Marital harmony ensured, Sir William returned to the mercenary. "Captain Crippen, I must ask, is this"—he held the letter up—"a jape? A jest? If so, 'tis a most poor one, indeed not one at all, that must end here, end now!" Behind Crippen, some of his men in warning jangled reins, bridles.

Crippen, hands up motioning for peace, shook his head, denying the accusation. "Sir William, your suspicions be understandable, but no, I assure you, there's no jest here, none!"

Still holding his hands up, he bent one wrist, index finger pointing. "That letter, Sir William, indeed comes from Grantville, there is indeed a Mistress Adina Daoud there, your missive and others do indeed come from her!" Slightly bowing head and torso now towards Sir William, he cautioned, "Sir William, she may well be a silly besom believing in ghosties and ghoulies, but her letters, to you, to others, are honestly meant!"

Slowly lowering his arms, he added, "And perhaps not so silly, figuring her letters would first be checked by the Westminster clerks!" With a slight shake of his head, he added, "I admit, on that she is most correct!"

Sir William stared into the captain's face, searching for levity. Seeing none, he considered the captain's words. "Others?" he asked.

"Oh, yes," Crippen stated fulsomely. "Others. For instance, one warns a man about his daughter, an ill-fated entanglement in a few years. Another, to the mayor and aldermen of Dunoon, about the inn at Loch Eck."

Sir William cocked his head. Ill-fated entanglements, well, yes, credit that Mistress Daoud with a plausibly believable tale there, but... "Captain Crippen, I've acquaintance of the Dunoon lands. There *is* no inn at Loch Eck. Cottages, naught more."

"True," admitted Crippen, unfazed. "There isn't one, as Mistress Daoud herself says. Writes. Not until 1650, though perhaps"—he shrugged—"sooner, now folk know there's money to be made there!"

Sir William again considered Crippen's words. No, those still made no sense. "As there is no inn, perhaps may never be, why write about its dwell-ins?"

"Dwell-in," corrected Crippen. "A small boy, who sleepwalks out the inn one night, drowning in the loch nearby. When found, his body was blue from the cold, hence the dwell-in, his ghost, was, is the Blue Boy. Sometimes, so Mistress Daoud wrote, watery footprints, little ones, are found on the inn floors."

Mien now equivocal, he added "She writes that should that inn be built, then guard against that. Lock doors, ask parents if their children sleepwalk. Sensible cautions, really." With that, he pointed anew to the letter in Sir William's left hand. "In truth, I say the same regarding hers to you, Sir William. Sensible cautions, sir, sensible cautions!"

Sir William, doubtful, asked, "You believe this—that tale, then?"

Crippen, considering Sir William's question, cautiously, carefully answered. "I believe tragedies happen, Sir William. Daughters, sons, choose—poorly. Guests murder, children wander, lovers die. Grief and despair—overwhelm. When and who, where, why, those change, but always, Sir William, always, at all times, in all places, tragedies happen."

Pausing, he finished with, "Whether dwell-ins, haunts, and ghosts exist, I don't know. Aye, the Bible says Saul spoke with the ghost of Samuel, but truly, I doubt any this side of the grave knows. But tragedies, Sir William, those I do know. Those exist. Always."

"Hmmm." Sir William inserted the letter back into its envelope. "You should stay a night in the Plaster Room, captain. That might assuage your doubts!" *Or increase them*, he thought, remembering his boyhood self sneaking from his bed to stay an hour in that room, half-fearing to meet the White Lady, to see Alice wandering the halls... Those roams never showed anything, but felt, oh yes...to this day sometimes, at night he felt...but Alice, the White Lady, or his own frights, he couldn't say.

Crippen's eyes widened. "Then, you do believe her?"

Sir William answered, "That, Captain Crippen, is best answered with your own words. I don't know! But yes, you are correct. Tragedies, those happen. Try as we might, as we do, tragedies happen. We plan, we prepare, 'Yet man is born unto trouble, as the sparks fly upward.' "

As Crippen nodded agreement to the words of Job, Sir William Davenport said, "Captain, the day is indeed long, night approaches. You and your men require shelter. There's a tithe barn a half-mile from here, the field lying fallow. Room enough and plenty for your men, your horses. Come with me, I will arrange good food and small beer—Dorothy makes an excellent one, from honey, rose-hips, and hops—"

Motioning the captain towards Bramall Hall, the fifth William Davenport requested, "Come, greet my wife, Captain. I believe—we should talk."

Bramall Hall
Some time later

"Your family really keeps people overnight in here, Peter?" asked a friend of young Davenport.

"Sometimes."

"Weird," voiced the friend.

"Totally weird," agreed Peter. "Windows bricked in, door locks on the outside—relax, I've a key, we can't be stuck inside!"

"Do they ever hold anybody—I mean, this isn't a room, Peter, it's a cell!" said another.

"No, never," said Peter. "We only lock them in overnight. Just for the night," he explained, adding, "And only unexpected ones, never people we know. You're safe!"

"What if there's a fire, or something?" asked a third.

"Yeah!" agreed another. "Or if they need a washroom, what then?"

Peter pointed to a chair, a hole in its seat, a bucket underneath, and nearby, a bag filled with raggy cloths, paper scraps. "That's the washroom right there, and if there's a fire"—Peter looked a little ill—"they just have to hope they get remembered in time, I guess."

"WEIRD," chorused the group.

Peter, shrugging, nodded agreement. "That it is, yet—we have our reasons for it!"

The State Library Papers
1632 Non-Fiction

Flint's Shards, Inc.

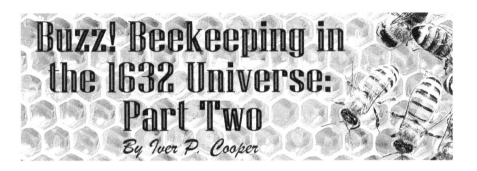

Buzz! Beekeeping in the 1632 Universe, Part 2

Iver P. Cooper

Transplanting Bees

T he European honey bee has been deliberately transported to regions outside its native range, notably North and South America, Australia and New Zealand, and Japan. There are obvious problems with shipping bees overseas on sailing ships. The voyages are long and there are no flowers from which to gather pollen or nectar. There is wind, sea spray and perhaps even waves, and poor ventilation below.

This section has several purposes. First, to point out where the bees were transplanted prior to the Ring of Fire, regardless of whether we know how this was accomplished. Second, to know how long, in time and distance, a passage could be survived. And finally, where possible, to know the particulars of the successful transport methods, even if those aren't documented in "Grantville literature."

Goodell found an 1830 description of a transport method, but it is not clear whether it was speculative or one actually carried out. This said that the hives were placed in a partitioned crate, one skep per compartment. The crate was bolted to a platform built at the stern of the ship, and the entrances of the hives were closed until the ship was out to sea. At that point the hives were reopened, and the bees could fly out through ventilation holes in the crate. However, unless some nectar source was provided outside the crate, it is not clear what the point of this would be (Borst).

Even if we don't know the particulars, it is good to at least know when the bees were embarked and how long the voyage took. That gives us some idea of the available technology, the bees' life expectancy, and the extent to which the bees' food stores would be depleted. A late fall or early winter departure would take advantage of the bees' normal seasonal round, in which they stop foraging and live longer.

New Spain

The situation in New Spain (Mexico and Central America) is muddled. In 1513, Herrera commented on the difficulty of transplanting honey bees to the "Indies." Brand asserted that the introduction probably occurred in the 1520s or 1530s, but Borst comments that this was based on the "flimsiest of evidence." He adds that the Spanish "successfully kept bees from being introduced into their colonies for many years. This apparently was done to guarantee the New World ecclesiastical candle wax market for beeswax produced in Spain" (Borst; Crane 361).

Bermuda

In 1616, Robert Rich wrote to his brother Nathaniel in England, "the bees that you sent do prosper very well" (Hilburn). (There were also bees, destined for Virginia, on the *Sea Venture*, which was shipwrecked in Bermuda in 1609, but I don't know whether those bees survived.)

Virginia

On December 5, 1621, the Council of the Virginia Company in London wrote to the Governor of Virginia, "We have by this ship and the Discouverie...sent you...beehives...." This is usually interpreted as meaning that the various goods listed were sent out on the *Discovery* (60 tons), which left in November 1621 and arrived in March 1622. However, it seems to me that the goods were on two ships, one of which was the *Discovery*, and the beehives might have been on either or both. The most likely candidates for the second ship were the *Bona Nova* (200 tons) which left and arrived a month later, and the *Hopewell* (60 tons), whose exact dates are not known (Kellar).

Massachusetts

The earliest date asserted for importation of bees to the Massachusetts Bay colony was 1638, but I have found no particulars. "In 1640 a town apiary was established in Danvers, Essex County.... Nathaniel Tilden...died in 1641" [and] "left ten stocks or swarms of bees, appraised at 10 pounds" (Crane 31).

Utah

The Mormons brought bees to Utah by wagon in 1848.

California

In 1853, Shelton purchased twelve hives from a beekeeper in Colon, Panama. They traveled by mule across the Isthmus, then by steamship to Alviso at the south end of San Francisco Bay, arriving in March. From there, they journeyed by train and mule to his ranch in Santa Clara County. "Only enough bees to form one hive survived." Shelton died a month later and his estate sold three hives "at auction for $110 each, 22 times the price of a beehive on the East Coast" (Riedy).

On October 29, 1857, Harbison, an experienced Pennsylvania beekeeper, left home with 67 hives. These were specially designed small (12x12x6 inches) box hives, one third the size of a normal box hive, with at least one comb containing worker eggs and young larvae placed in each box, together with adult bees, in June. Thus, there was time for each of these divides to rear a queen, for the queen to mate, and a brood to begin. Shortly before departure, a hole was cut in the side of the box hive and a box (3x6x12 inches) with wire screen over the ends tacked over the hole. The purpose was to offer increased ventilation and a place to cast out dead bees. The box hives had flat tops and bottoms so they could be staked together, and the total weight came to 1,303 pounds. The bees first traveled by wagon, boat and train to New York City. On November 5, they sailed on the *Northern Light*. They were "placed on the top (hurricane) deck where they were securely tied with an oilcloth cover fitted over each package to protect them from the rains and salt spray, while an awning was stretched overhead to shield the hives from the direct rays of the sun...." After ten days at sea, they arrived at Aspinwall, Panama. There the bees were allowed to fly. The next day, they were loaded on a train to Panama City, where they were transferred to the steamship *Sonora*. It left on November 16, and arrived at San Francisco November 30. The bees were then transferred to a river steamer, arriving in Sacramento on December 2. In five hives the bees were dead, and twelve were so weak that he transferred the survivors to the remaining fifty hives. The latter sold for $100 apiece.

He repeated the process the following year, leaving his farm November 15, and New York City December 6, arriving in Sacramento December 31, 1858. This time, he used a Langstroth-type hive, and there was no "sightseeing" day in Aspinwall. While "there were many dead bees in each hive, only 11 of the 114 hives were completely dead" (Watkins).

Hawaii

The first two attempts at transplantation were unsuccessful. In 1852, a ship sailed to Honolulu from Boston, but the honeycomb melted in the tropics. In 1853, the hives were packed in ice, but that replaced one problem with another. In 1857, four hives were successfully shipped to Hawaii from California (Kim).

Australia

In 1806, Blaxland requested cargo space on the *William Pitt* for "a swarm of bees in cabin with wire cage over the hive," but "there is no evidence the bees were ever taken on board." There were unsuccessful attempts to bring honey bees to Australia in 1809 and 1821. In the first case, the bees died from heat exposure when crossing the Equator. In the second, the bees died soon after arrival (Barrett). The consensus is that the first successful transplantation was by the *Isabella*, which left Cork on November 4, 1821 and arrived on March 11, 1822 (a 125-day passage) (Willetts). On March 14, 1822, "seven hives of bees, just imported from England," were advertised for auction (Barrett). Note that this is autumn in Australia, and so it wouldn't have been easy for the bees to survive the coming winter with their food stores already depleted during the passage.

More hives arrived on the *Phoenix*, which left Portsmouth March 29, 1823 and arrived in Hobart, Tasmania, July 21, 1824 (114-day passage), and then in Sydney in August (Barrett). That being austral winter, again the bees might not have survived.

Perhaps the first truly successful introduction was by Thomas Braidwood Wilson, surgeon of the *John*. It left Spithead October 14, 1830, and arrived in Hobart January 28, 1831 (106 days). In February, it was reported that his bees "are now in the Government Garden, and being let loose from the wire cage that surrounded them during the voyage, roam at large among the few flowers and blossoms that still afford them food though at this late period of the season" (vandemonian).

Neighbour (213) sent bees from London to Australia by steamship on September 25, 1862 (79-day passage). These were Italian bees, in Woodbury frame hives. They relied on their own food supply but water was supplied to them during the voyage. Hives were later sent by sailing ship, but only one of four survived—Neighbour says because of water supply mismanagement.

New Zealand

Two skeps of honey bees were brought by Mary Bumby in a five-month voyage, arriving March 1839 (Middleditch).

Japan

European honey bees (Italian subspecies) were imported in 1877 (Yoshiyama).

Pollination

Pollination—the transfer of pollen from the anthers (male part) of a plant to the stigma (female part) of a plant of the same species—is an essential part of plant reproduction. With most plant species, both self-pollination and cross-pollination are possible.

"Since bees tend to focus on collecting pollen from one flower species at a time, there is a high probability that they will transfer it either to the stigma of the same flower or to that of another flower of the same species" (Wilson-Rich 49).

Bees are not the only pollinators, and honey bees are not the only bees. But honey bees are numerically abundant, super-generalist pollinators.

Migratory Beekeeping

This is the practice of transporting beehives from one farm to another to pollinate the crops. They are delivered to the field just before the plants flower. With adequate transportation, bees can be kept active year round, moving north in the summer and south in the winter.

A small-scale example of migratory beekeeping is found in Scotland, where beekeepers "move colonies to the heather moorlands in August to get crops of" ling heather honey. There was a similar practice in Zelem, Belgium: "when beekeepers took hives into an area in the spring (to prepare for the heather later), they had to pay the lord 3 groats per hive...." (Crane 447). And the large-scale example is the movement of "1.5 million hives to California Central Valley almond groves" for pollination purposes (Seeley 94).

The first experiments began in the 1870s, and the beehives were moved by river barge and rail cars. This was not practical because the hives had to be offloaded and transported to the fields by horse and wagon (Rucker 11). In modern practice, the hives are kept on pallets, and the pallets are moved onto flatbed trucks by a forklift. Unfortunately, this ease of operation has led to a rise in "hive theft" (Zaleski).

Beekeeping and the Law

Roman Law

Both Anglo-American common law and European civil law have antecedents in Roman law. Roman jurists attempted to draw a distinction between domesticated animals and wild animals (*ferae naturae* or *ferae bestiae*). With a domesticated animal, if it wandered off your land, it remained your property. But a wild animal was owned by no one (*res nullius*) until one gained control over it (*occupatio*). Originally, the control had to be physical—enclosure—and if the animal escaped, you no longer owned it. But it was recognized that the control could be psychological—taming the animal (*mansuetae*). As a practical matter, to be considered tame, the animal had to have the habit of returning home (*animus revertendi*). If so, the individual animal was treated as domesticated even though it belonged to a species that was normally wild.

Pliny the Elder, an early naturalist, suggested that some animals, including bees, were "neither tame nor wild, but of an intermediate nature." This was rejected by Gaius. "Because bees have a wild nature, they do not become ours when they settle on our tree, but only when we have shut them into our hive."

But Gaius did agree that once hived (and until they swarm), bees have an "intent to return" (*animus revertendi*). But what about swarming bees? Gaius' general rule was that a wild animal held captive recovered its liberty when "it escapes from our vision, or, although it may be in our sight, its pursuit is difficult" (Gaius, Institutes, 2:67). (Frier says this refers to physical difficulty.) And so the swarm was treated like a wild animal that was attempting escape.

Anglo-American Law

The common law on establishing ownership in bees is a bit muddled. Bracton (early thirteenth century) wrote, referencing one of Gaius' similes, "though a swarm lights upon my tree, I have no more property in them till I have hived them, than I have in the birds which make their nests thereon; and therefore if another hives them, he shall be their proprietor..."

However, the Charter of the Forest (1217) declared that "every freeman shall have...the honey that is found within his own woods." (The bees might disagree.) And based on this, Blackstone (1760s) argued that "a qualified property may be had in bees, in consideration of the property of the soil whereon they are found."

Some cases have drawn a distinction between a swarm of bees that is temporarily resting on the branches of a tree, and those that have made a home in it. The latter, the court said, should belong to the landowner "in the same manner and for the same reason as all mines and minerals belong to the owner of the soil" (Trusler 48).

What if someone other than the landowner hives the bees? According to some nineteenth-century American cases (Trusler), if that person has a right to be on the land (e.g., a tenant farmer), the hiving confers title. But a trespasser gains no rights by this industry. That's true even if the trespasser was the one who found the bees.

What if the bees, once hived, should swarm and leave one's land? Blackstone says, "a swarm, which flie from and out of my hive, are mine so long as I can keep them in sight, and have power to pursue them; and in these circumstances no one else is entitled to take them." That includes the owner of the land that they moved to, and the pursuer need only keep them in sight until they settle. The catch is that following them onto someone else's land without permission is still trespass. In *Kearry v. Pattinson* (1939), Judge Goddard said that the landowner could lawfully refuse to give the pursuer that permission and that such refusal terminated the pursuer's ownership. Judge Slesser went a step further: he held "power to pursue" meant "lawful power" and thus ownership terminated as soon as the bees entered another's land (SCS).

We turn next to the issue of whether the beekeeper is liable if the bees injure another person, or another person's property (livestock). One who owns a wild animal is strictly liable for any harm the animal causes. Bees, however, are treated like domestic animals, so there is normally liability only in the case of negligence "in the number kept, in their management or the location of their hives" (Trusler).

However, again as in the case of domestic animals, the bee owner is strictly liable after being put on notice that the animal has "vicious propensities." Such notice could be provided by the past conduct of the bees, i.e., a previous unprovoked attack. (Some courts might, instead of invoking strict liability, hold that this past conduct elevates the required standard of care to avoid liability for negligence.)

* * *

The West Virginia Apiary Law of 1991 provided that beekeepers must register annually, and that all colonies of honey bees would be inspected by the State for the presence of disease or parasites. If they were found, and treatment was possible, it had to be carried out within fourteen days of notice, and in the meantime a quarantine was imposed. Otherwise, the colonies were depopulated without remuneration and the hives and equipment destroyed or sterilized. Bees, or used hives and equipment, could not be brought into the state without a suitable certificate of inspection from the state of origin, and the grant of a permit of entry. The State also was given power to establish an exterior quarantine to prevent diseased or parasitized bees and related equipment from being transported into West Virginia. The statute also prohibited the use, inconsistent with the labeling, of pesticides injurious to bees to treat agricultural crops in full bloom. Both civil and criminal liability were possible for various violations of the law (WV 1991).

While the laws of West Virginia came through the Ring of Fire—see *The Persistence of Dreams*, Chapter 1—we have the curious situation that the only person in Grantville who is a beekeeper is also the only person conceivably qualified to serve as an inspector. *Quis custodiet ipso custodes?*

German Law

In 1350, Charles IV granted the forest beekeepers the right to collect honey in the forest area around Nürnberg, with the understanding that they were to supply some honey to the emperor. In 1427, the forest was sold to the city of Nürnberg (Schamberger).

The current German Civil Law is clearly derived from the Roman law. The relevant provisions are (mythomane):

Section 961: Where a swarm of bees takes flight, it becomes ownerless if the owner fails to pursue it without undue delay or if he gives up the pursuit.

Section 962: The owner of the swarm of bees may, in pursuit, enter on plots of land belonging to others. If the swarm has entered an unoccupied beehive belonging to another, the owner of the swarm, for the purpose of capturing it, may open the hive and remove or break out the combs. He must make compensation for the damage caused.

Section 963: If bee swarms of more than one owner that have moved out merge, the owners who have pursued their swarms become co-owners of the total swarm captured; the shares are determined according to the number of swarms pursued.

Section 964: If a bee swarm has moved into an occupied beehive belonging to another, the ownership and the other rights in the bees that were occupying the beehive extend to the swarm that has moved in. The ownership and the other rights in the swarm that has moved in are extinguished.

Other Legal Frameworks

I have only uncovered fragmentary references to the laws of other lands. In general they seem to give the landowner control even over wild bees.

"In Zelem [Belgium] in 1486 the lord had the right to take half of any swarm found, or a tax of 1 shilling or more. All swarms had to be reported to the bailiff, and the penalty for not doing so was confiscation of the swarm" (Crane 447).

"Russian princes owned vast bee forests in which the largest trees were protected by law to provide homes for honey bees" (Seeley 24).

In Malaysia, since the twelfth century, the honey hunters have needed the sultan's permission each year to harvest honey from the forest around Pedu Lake (Buchmann 98).

Conclusion

Beekeeping may seem a more prosaic subject for 1632 universe stories than ironclads, airships and airplanes, or oil drilling, but by the same token, it is one that does not require advanced up-time knowledge to become involved in.

One can envision many ways in which a character's involvement in beekeeping can drive a story: the competition of honey with the slavery-associated cane sugar, the humanitarian quest to replace traditional "swarm" beekeeping with moveable frame beekeeping, conflicts between beekeepers and their neighbors or feudal lords, and so forth.

Note: The bibliography for this article (and indeed for all my articles) will be posted to my subdomain, iver1632.myartsonline.com and/or to https://author.1632magazine.com/getting-started/writer-resources/.

Appendix 1: More Up-Timer/Beekeepers?

While the rules of the 1632 universe prohibit giving any up-timer a pre-Ring of Fire occupation of beekeeping who wasn't given it originally, authors are free to assign beekeeping as a hobby to their claimed up-timer characters, assuming that the total number so assigned remains reasonable.

The West Virginia Beekeepers Association was founded in 1917. It has a Master Beekeeper program, with three levels: Apprentice, Certified (requires three years' experience and two blue ribbons at honey shows), and Master (five years' experience and a honey show judge). Completing the two higher levels required public service, such as assisting members of youth organizations (4-H, Scouts, FFA). There is also, specifically, a Marion County Beekeepers Association, and it was founded in 1971, in Fairmont (MCBA). A 2010 WV Department of Agriculture report notes that the MCBA had been holding "a beginner's beekeeping class every year for over 20 years...." (Martel).

Grantville is modeled on real-life Mannington, West Virginia, which is in Marion County. The Marion County Beekeepers Association's current facebook group has 331 members (some of whom may actually live "out of county"). The 2019 population of Marion County was 56,072 (Wikipedia). If we assume that 3500 people were picked up by the Ring of Fire, and that the ratio of beekeepers to total population was the same as the ratio of the present MCBA facebook group membership to the 2019 Marion County population, that would imply that there were 21 beekeepers in Grantville as of the Ring of Fire. But it is also possible that beekeeping is just a lot more popular now than it was then.

According to the 2007 Census of Agriculture, West Virginia in 2002 had 411 farms with colonies of bees, from which 310,228 pounds of honey were collected. And the 2012 Census reported that in 2012 West Virginia had 919 farms, with 9325 colonies, and 326,048 pounds were collected from 550 farms. The same year, Marion County had 22 farms, with 68 colonies, and 12 of the farms collected honey, collecting a total of 2,306 pounds. Given that Marion County has a population sixteen times that of the Ring of Fire, and a land area about eleven times that, this would imply that there were only one or two farms with beekeepers in the Ring of Fire circle in 2012.

So, depending on what statistics we extrapolate from, there might be anywhere from one to a score of amateur beekeepers in pre-Ring of Fire Grantville.

I would guess that the most likely candidates for hobbyist beekeepers would be those with a pre-Ring of Fire employment as farmers (there weren't many in Grantville) and those already identified in the Grid as having gardening as a hobby. Willie Ray Hudson and Andy Parlow each have a B.S. in Agriculture. George Trimble, Jr. (1964-) was a farmer. Carlyle Johnson (1925-1635), Orville Mobley (1933-1637), Harry Wright (1934-1638) and John Straley (1912-1636) were retired farmers. The Garden Club members were Linda Jane Freeman (1960-), Mildred Jenkins (1935-), Delia Ruggles (1941-), Irma Vandine Lawler (1928-), and Alden Williams, Sr. (1952-), but Miriam Nassif (1933-), Amy Jo Prickett (1978-), and Jewel Torbert (1934-) also gardened.

There was a Boy Scout merit badge in beekeeping from 1911 to 1995 (Lewis). There was a Girl Scout beekeeper merit badge 1947-1963 (Worthpoint).

Appendix 2: Grantville Literature

Daphne Pridmore was presumably an MCBA member and therefore could have borrowed and taken notes on books from their library—see the list here but ignore anything published after 1999!

The current reading list for the WVBA beekeeper examinations is here https://drive.google.com/file/d/1WY5If3RKB9ioewMbUm5ykdBG -wevOBGV/view

I would assume that her knowledge of bees and beekeeping is at least equivalent to PennState's *Beekeeping Basics* (2004), the currently required apprentice text, although she would have obtained her knowledge from an older source (possibly the 1978, 1986, or 1998 edition of Sammataro, *The Beekeeper's Handbook*). To have qualified as a Master Beekeeper by 1999, she would have had to start in 1994 or earlier, i.e., age 21 or younger. That's certainly possible. There's nothing in the grid to indicate that anyone from her parents' or grandparents' generation was a beekeeper, which reduces the chance that she started working with bees as a child.

Besides whatever books and videos Daphne Pridmore (and any other hobbyist beekeepers) may have accumulated, there is information on late nineteenth-/early twentieth-century practice in the 1911 *Encyclopedia Britannica* (EB11), "Bee." Late twentieth-century practice is described, at least superficially, in recent encyclopedias. The only one I consulted was the 2002 CD-ROM edition (EB2002CD) of the *Encyclopedia Britannica*, which is based on the 1999 print edition.

The North Marion High School library has Hoyt, *The World of Bees* (1965). Mannington Public Library has Adams, *Beekeeping: The Gentle Craft* (1988). We do not know what pre-2000 books may have been discarded.

News and New Books
Available Now and Coming Soon

Flint's Shards, Inc.

Inside Baseball
Bjorn Hasseler

Since Robert finished his Cassini cycle of baseball stories in this issue, I decided on a baseball name for this column. It's the inside scoop, the nuts and bolts, perhaps a little of how the sausage is made.

Most of the staff of *Eric Flint's 1632 & Beyond* just got home from Libertycon. While it wasn't the 1632 con for the year, it's very Baen-adjacent. We did have a 1632 panel. We talked about novels, novels, and this magazine.

When I try to explain what's in the Assiti Shards universes to someone who hasn't read them, I find it's a lot.

In the 1632 universe, there are:

27 novels from Baen. Sometimes you'll hear these described as "mainline" novels, but that's not technically correct. Eric defined the mainline novels as those a) dealing with high politics and featuring more than one of the four original couples from *1632* (Mike & Rebecca, Gretchen & Jeff, James Nichols & Melissa Mailey, Julie & Alex). So the mainline is *1632, 1633, 1634: The Baltic War, 1635: The Eastern Front, 1636: The Saxon Uprising, 1636: The Ottoman Onslaught, 1637: The Polish Maelstrom,* and *1637: The Transylvanian Decision.*

2 themed anthologies from Baen. The stories in *1634: The Ram Rebellion* and *1637: The Coast of Chaos* are so closely linked that I usually group them with the novels, but others may prefer to count them differently.

4 *Ring of Fire* anthologies from Baen. These are stories that did not appear in any magazine.

9 *Grantville Gazette* anthologies from Baen. These use Roman numerals. I-IV match the magazine issues, with the addition of a new story by Eric in each. V-IX are best-of collections, each spanning an increasing number of *Gazette* issues.

46 books from Ring of Fire press. These tend to be shorter than the Baen novels and are often in the 70,000- to 90,000-word range. One was a themed non-fiction collection, one was a themed anthology, and the other 44 were novels or single-author collections. Content varied from simply combining all the parts of a serial from various *Gazette* issues to novels that were entirely new material. Baen has acquired approximately 20 of these plus 2 more that were in the on-deck circle, as it were, and is reissuing one per month as an ebook.

102 issues of the *Grantville Gazette* magazine.

This is Issue 6 of *Eric Flint's 1632 & Beyond* magazine.

Then there are the other four Assiti Shards. We'll talk about those another time.

It works out to at least 14,000,000 words and 201 authors.

Canon is a term for what's recognized as official. Novels and anthologies from Baen are canon. Magazine stories are provisionally canon and are confirmed once they're selected for an anthology. That is, if there's a problem, a Baen book takes precedence over a magazine story. Any new stories need to be in continuity with books and magazine stories that have been previously published. Please note that does not mean a potential author needs to read everything in the 1632 universe before writing a story. If you have a topic in mind, we can suggest a reading list.

Available Now

The Trouble with Huguenots, The
Carthaginian Crisis, Legions of Pestilence,
Security Solutions, Security Threats,
Missions of Security

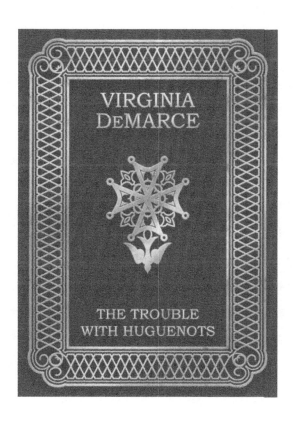

The Trouble with Huguenots
Virginia DeMarce

Ever since the assassination of King Louis XIII and the overthrow of his chief minister, Cardinal Richelieu, France has been in political and military turmoil. The possibility—even the likelihood—of revolution hovers in the background. The new king Gaston, whom many consider an usurper, is no friend of France's Protestants, known as the Huguenots. The fears and hostility of the Huguenots toward the French crown have only been heightened by the knowledge brought back in time by the Americans of the town of Grantville. Half a century in the future, the French king of the time would revoke the Edict of Nantes of 1598, which proclaimed that the rights of Huguenots would be respected. At the center of all this turmoil is the universally recognized leader of the Huguenots: Duke Henri de Rohan. He knows from the same up-time history books that he is "scheduled" to die less than two years in the future and he has pressing problem on his hands. His estranged wife and brother are siding with the usurper Gaston and plotting against him. Still worse, his sole child and heir is his nineteen-year-old daughter Marguerite. He believes he has less than two years to find a suitable husband for her—but acceptable Calvinist noblemen, French or foreign, are sparse at the moment. What's a father to do?

https://www.baen.com/the-trouble-with-huguenots-demarce.html

*"The Trouble with Huguenots" by
Virginia DeMArce*

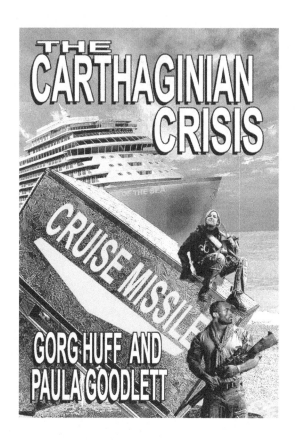

The Carthaginian Crisis
Gorg Huff and Paula Goodlett

Antigonus One-eye has murdered Susan Godlewski. He did it on camera as a political statement of dominance. The Ship People, the people from the twenty-first century who had arrived in this time on the Cruise ship Queen of the Sea, had to respond. Or they would be the meat for any bandit chief from the tag end of the fourth century BCE.

Captain Lars Floden declared Antigonus One-eye dead, but despite the magical beliefs of this time, just saying it didn't make it so. Making it so would demand courage, and commitment, misdirection, and impossible technology from the twenty-first century. As well as time and more than a little luck.

In the meantime, Ptolemy has decided that he wants more than Egypt. He wants Sicily and its highly productive farms. If Carthage wants to argue the point, well he'll take Carthage too.

Carthage is in a panic. It can't abandon its allies on Sicily. To do so would be to destroy its trading empire. They have a strong and capable navy. Better now that they have been able to buy steam engines from the ship people. However their army is mostly mercenaries. Mercenaries who won't stand up to Ptolemy.

Ptolemy doesn't need control of the Mediterranean to conquer Carthage. He can march an army along the north coast of Africa. Carthage needs allies, and fear of what Ptolemy might do to them is forcing them to consider the brand new Pax Romana.

This is the fourth book in the Queen of the Sea series. "The Alexander Inheritance" and "The Macedonian Hazard" were published by Baen, "The Sicilian Coil" which discussed what was happening in Western Europe, while "The Macedonian Hazard" was dealing with Eastern Europe, was published by Ring of Fire Press. Then after Ring of Fire Press folded self-published by Paula and I on Amazon. This book "The Carthaginian Crisis" continues the universe almost from the moment of the end of "The Sicilian Coil" and combines the two narratives while adding other threads.

This is the next book in the Queen of the Sea series but not the last. Like the 1632 series, The Queen of the Sea is an open ended series with lots of room to grow.

https://www.amazon.com/gp/product/B0D771S6TB?ref_=dbs_m_mng_rwt_calw_tkin_1&storeType=ebooks&qid=1719540801&sr=1-1

"The Carthaginian Crisis" by
Gorg Huff and Paula Goodlett

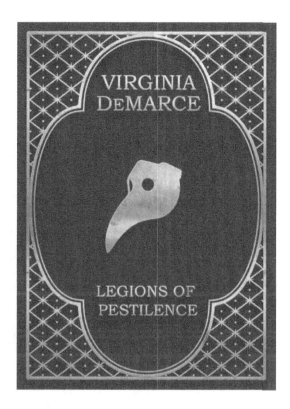

Legions of Pestilence
Virginia DeMarce

"In the world the West Virginians of Grantville came from, the borderlands between France and Germany had been a source of turmoil for centuries. In the new universe created by the Ring of Fire, the situation isn't any better. The chaotic condition of the German lands has been ended--for a time, at least. And the near-century long war between Spain and the Netherlands has finally been resolved.

But now France is unstable. The defeat of Richelieu's forces in the Ostend War has weakened the Red Cardinal's grip on political power and emboldened his enemies, Foremost among them is King Louis XIII's ambitious younger brother, Monsieur Gaston. An inveterate schemer and would-be usurper, Gaston's response to the new conditions in France is to launch a military adventure. He invades the Duchy of Lorraine. Soon, others are drawn into the conflict. The Low Countries ruled by King Ferdinand and Duke Bernhard's newly formed Burgundy, a kingdom-in-all-but-name, send their own troops into Lorraine. Chaos expands and spreads up and down the Rhine.

It isn't long before the mightiest and most deadly army enters the fray--the legions of pestilence. Bubonic plague and typhus lead the way, but others soon follow: dysentery, deadly and disfiguring smallpox, along with new diseases introduced by the time-displaced town of Grantville. The war is on. All the wars--and on all fronts. Can the medical knowledge of the up-time Americans be adapted and spread fast enough to forestall disaster? Or will their advanced military technology simply win one war in order to lose the other and much more terrible one?"

Available here:

https://www.baen.com/legions-of-pestilence.html

"Legions of Pestilence" by Virginia DeMarce

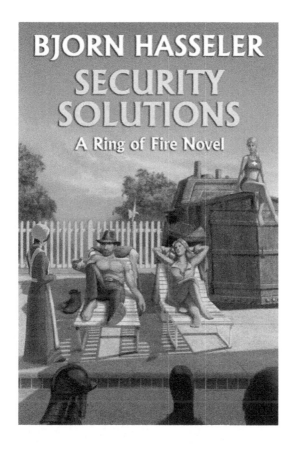

Security Solutions
Bjorn Hasseler

When the Ring of Fire drags Grantville, West Virginia, back to seventeenth-century Germany, down-time veteran Edgar Neustatter finds himself among the survivors of a unit devastated by the up-time Americans and their Swedish allies. Soon, he establishes a new agency: Neustatter's European Security Services.

Security Solutions is the fourth book in the NESS series, after *A Matter of Security*, *Missions of Security*, and *Security Threats*.

Available here:

https://www.baen.com/security-solutions.html

*"Security Solutions" by Bjorn Has-
seler*

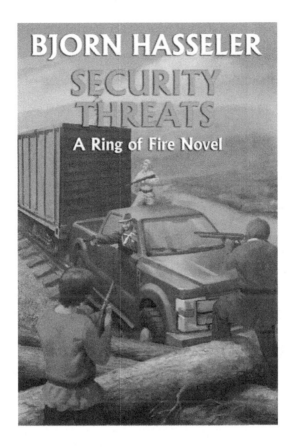

Security Threats
Bjorn Hasseler

Neustatter's European Security Services encounters a campaign of industrial sabotage, a pastor who attempts to limit their client base, an espionage ring, and the aftermath of the Dreeson assassination. Old nemeses and new allies complicate matters.

Somewhere in Grantville is a missing heiress. There's also a Resistance, and it has cookies. Even repeat business with established clients is complicated, not to mention dangerous. Real life proves more complicated than

Neustatter's movies or Astrid's books as NESS looks for common threads. Which incidents are related and which are not?

For Astrid Schäubin, solving cases, directing operations, and even portraying a saint are one thing, but figuring out dating in the midst of everything that's happening is quite another.

Security Threats is the third book in the NESS series, after *A Matter of Security* and *Missions of Security*.

Available here:

https://www.baen.com/security-threats.html

"Security Threats" by Bjorn Hasseler

Missions of Security
Bjorn Hasseler

Neustatter's European Security Services is open for business, and business is . . . *too* good?

With the National Guard, private industry, and even a seemingly tranquil farming village caught in an explosive political crossroads all relying on NESS for missions of security, Neustatter and Astrid find themselves pressed to staff, train, and equip the agency while keeping up with their clients' growing requirements in scope and complexity.

-- A simple railway escort mission involves a secretive manufacturing client from Grantville bearing mysterious cargo and a captured fugitive all destined for Magdeburg during the Baltic War . . . what could possibly go wrong?

-- The Bible Society hires NESS to guard a flock of Anabaptist, Catholic, and Lutheran high schoolers *en route* to riot-torn Erfurt and Jena, but will NESS's own pastor tear them apart first?

-- Already strapped for personnel, the last thing Neustatter needs is for a regiment of dragoon militia to choose their wagon train for . . . "involuntary provisioning." Can a handful of badly outnumbered agents protect a village that isn't sure it wants their help?

Missions of Security is the sequel to *A Matter of Security*, and contains the full text of the previously published short story, "Blood in Erfurt."

Available here:

https://www.baen.com/missions-of-security.html

"Missions of Security" by Bjorn Hasseler

Coming Soon
Things Could be Worse, Designed to Fail, 1635: The Weaver's Code

Things Could be Worse
Virginia DeMarce

The Ring of Fire that transported the town of Grantville from West Virginia in the year 2000 to the region of Thuringia in the middle of Europe in the year 1631 produced an enormous cascade of changes in world history. Some of those changes were big, others were huge—and some were more modest in scale. Modest, at the least, to the universe, if not necessarily to those immediately affected.

Count Ludwig Guenther of Schwarzburg-Rudolstadt builds a Lutheran church on his own land, not far from Grantville, and calls in a Saxon pastor of a Phillipist bent to serve the Lutheran refugee population of the area. Shortly thereafter, in April 1634, the pastor's older daughter meets and elopes with a Catholic up-timer, which prompts Kastenmayer to get Lutheran girls to marry unchurched up-timers and thereby recruit them into the parish.

In the years that follow, Pastor Kastenmayer copes with both existing ecclesio-political strands of down-time religion (from Stiefelite Lutheran heretics to Flacian Lutheran ultra-orthodox) and the strange new up-time world of shorts, blue jeans, and unknown religious denominations. His struggles and travails have a surprisingly revolutionary impact on seventeenth-century Lutheranism—perhaps to no one's greater surprise than the pastor himself.

https://www.baen.com/things-could-be-worse-demarce.html

Full book available August 6

*"Things Could be Worse" by Vir-
ginia DeMarce*

Designed to Fail
Virginia DeMarce

Frederik of Denmark, the son of King Christian IV, is the new governor of the new province of Westphalia and harbors the dark suspicion that the Swedes who now dominate central Europe deliberately designed the province so that he would not succeed in his assignment, thus undermining his father's position. Problems are everywhere! Religious fragmentation, cities demanding imperial status, jurisdictional disputes among the nobility and between the nobility and the common folk—there's no end to it.

And then matters get still more complicated. Annalise Richter, a student at the famous Abbey of Quedlinburg, wants Frederik to correct an injustice. Her mentor, the Abbess of Quedlinburg, is being prevented from running for a seat in the House of Commons because she is, well, not a commoner. Surely Frederik can do something to fix this wrong! The prince is of two minds. On the one hand—being very much his father's son—he has developed a great passion for the marvelous young woman. He is determined to marry her. On the other hand . . . she's Catholic. A bit of a problem, that, for a Lutheran prince. But there's worse. She's also the younger sister of Gretchen Richter. Yes, that Gretchen Richter.

https://www.baen.com/designed-to-fail.html

Full book available September 3

*"Designed to Fail" by Virginia
DeMarce*

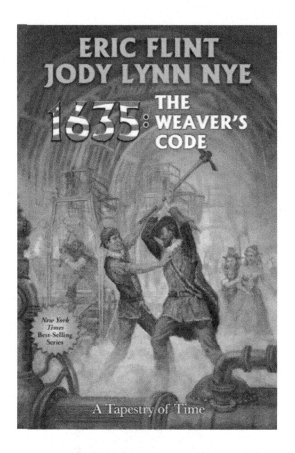

1635: The Weaver's Code
Eric Flint and Jody Lynn Nye

A young gentlewoman, Margaret de Beauchamp, finds her fate twisted into the lives of the up-timers when she meets the Americans imprisoned in the Tower of London. In exchange for her help, Rita Simpson and Harry Lefferts give her a huge sum of money to keep her family's manor and its woolen trade from falling into the hands of the crown and its unscrupulous minister, Lord Cork. But Margaret's troubles are not at an end. Her family's fortunes are in a downward spiral. Her trip to Grantville brings unexpected dangers and a possible up-time solution.

Inspired by books in the Grantville library, Margaret has an idea to restore her family's fortunes with an innovation never before seen in fabric design. With the help of Aaron Craig, an up-timer programmer using aqualators, water-powered computers, they teach her father's craftsmen to create a combination machine loom that can produce a new type of woolen cloth. The ornate and perfect patterns quickly trend among the nobility. However, the Master Weavers of the county's Weaver's Guild aren't happy about being overshadowed by the changes to the status quo, and take their grievance to Lord Cork, who is still looking for the people who helped the Americans escape from the Tower.

Cork isn't interested in squabbles between mere tradesmen, but he is very interested in taking over the new calculating machine that is fueling the upsurge in the de Beauchamp fortunes. He sends agents ordered to stop at nothing to secure it for his own ends. Margaret has to protect her new business, and prevent anyone from discovering that up-timers are in the country to assist her, but she still has to deal with an uprising at home.

https://www.baen.com/1635-the-weaver-s-code.html

https://www.amazon.com/1635-Weavers-Code-Ring-Fire/dp/198219 3662/ref=tmm_hrd_swatch_0?_encoding=UTF8&dib_tag=se&dib=eyJ 2IjoiMSJ9.ao1pVNDpv8-7LEpmWT_egg.uOgQWmD_nhRTh0o1bv HjvDXLd_QIVkCBB21qH5PFlTA&qid=1719541651&sr=8-1

Coming October 1

*"1635: The Weaver's Code" by
Eric Flint and Jody Lynn Nye*

Connect with Eric Flint's 1632 & Beyond

We would love to hear from you here at *Eric Flint's 1632 & Beyond!* There are lots of ways to get in touch with us and we look forward to hearing from you.

Main Sites

Email: 1632Magazine@1632Magazine.com

Shop: 1632Magazine.com

Author Site: Author.1632Magazine.com

For anyone interested in writing in the 1632verse, or fans interested in more background on the series and how we keep track of everything.

Social Media

Our Facebook Group is our primary social media, but we do use the FB Page, YouTube, and Instagram accounts.

Facebook Group: The Grantville Gazette / 1632 & Beyond

YouTube: 1632andBeyond

Facebook Page: Facebook.com/t1632andBeyond

Reviews and More

Because reviews really do matter, especially for small publishers and indie authors, please take a few minutes to post a review online or wherever you find books, and don't forget to tell your friends to check us out!

You are welcome to join us on **BaensBar.net**. Most of the chatting about 1632 on the Bar is in the 1632 Tech forum. If you want to read and comment on possible future stories, check out 1632 Slush (stories) and 1632 Slush Comments on BaensBar.net.

If you are interested in writing in the 1632 universe, that's fabulous! Please visit **Author.1632Magazine.com** (QR code above) for more information.

Made in the USA
Las Vegas, NV
08 June 2025

23342524R00098